Dear __

Thank you for your beautiful letter.

I'm upset. I can't justify what I did, or defend myself. I realize you aren't attacking.

I understand why you're mad at me, I understand exactly. It's not just that I wrote a novel about you, about your boyfriend, intruding on you guys' privacy. It's that I wrote about somebody too fragile to take it. That I risked his life.

I risked your boyfriend's sanity and life for the sake of me putting out a book, for the sake of stupid ART.

And any day he may still go out and buy the book and read it. It could still relapse him!

I just don't have an answer. I'm not a good friend to have, because I'll write about exactly what's

worst screwedup in our lives, and
then I'll be morally obtuse about
the consequences.

(I'm not used to anybody READING me
yet.)

But "morally obtuse" doesn't do it.
Cause see, I was only obtuse WHILE
I was writing--while writing the
book I really didn't see any problem!

Then I gave it to you, and you
stopped talking to me. Revelation,
I went "OH--I guess I wrote a dam-
aging dangerous thing. But at least
I won't ever publish it."

Then I went ahead and PUBLISHED IT
ANYWAY. That was interesting, huh?
I went right past "morally obtuse"
into "fucked."

One of the fuckeder things is how I
decided I'd protect him from the
book by having you "screen" it for
him. I forgot to protect YOU. Knew
better than to believe in your fake
role as all-tough wife, passer-of-
all-tests, never-bleeder girl. That

face you struggle to keep cool for his sake.

What's really fab is that <u>I would do it all again</u>! I would write the thing, and this time I'd try some trick way to slip it past you so you don't get hurt--but I would still write it and print it.

So what's that mean? Friends are expendable?

It means I'm trying to work. I want to be exempt from social niceties <u>within my work</u>. You do art by look-ing at what stuff is bothering you, and you dig into it, and maybe that gets you in trouble. But writing bargain says if you're really hon-est in your work, then even the trouble it gets you in will be the portals of discovery, and in the long run be worth it.

I'm sorry I made you miserable. If I blew out our friendship forever, then I'm paying very high for just a book, cause you both are impor-tant to me.

<u>Please call me up</u>, OK? I miss you.

Love,

Jim.

Wow. Not even close.

Can't I get myself off the hook with one sludgy letter? No. It'll take a whole new book of excuses.

Yes I actually had the nerve to write her that "portals of discovery, in the long run worth it." Worth the "trouble" *I* get in with her, when because of me her *boyfriend* maybe commits suicide! Hey he's dead but let's be fair, the novel's still excellent. Six dollars postpaid.

And I'd do it all again.

In Candyland it's cool to feed on your friends

Other lovely novels by James Albion Chapman:

Our plague: a film from New York

The walls collide as you expand, dwarf maple

Glass (pray the electrons back to sand)

In Candyland it's cool to feed on your friends

James Chapman

fugue state press
new york

Copyright © 1997 by James Chapman

Library of Congress
Catalog Card Number 96-83214

ISBN 1-879193-05-1

A portion of this book originally
appeared in *Central Park*.

Illustrations: Valery Carrick

Manufactured in the United States of America

Published by Fugue State Press
P.O. Box 80, Cooper Station
New York NY 10276

for randie

Why do you attack and hurt your friends?

Because that's where the love is stored.

Between us is a story. That means, between us a memory of wrongdoing.

Like say I take a picture of you. The picture's you being you in your chair, looking reply equally, you're watching me watch,

(photograph tall girl sweatshirt calm holding basketball and looking back into our eyes)

doesn't matter what feeling your face shows or tries to not

(same girl, tugging down at sweatshirt, one eye shut skeptical)

or (girl, directly pissed-off)

even (her mouth open, face snarled-up, hand grabbing out at camera eye)—even then *fighting* we made the picture together, we're friends living our lives, that's one kind of picture.

The other kind of picture—

(in the dark corner by the radiator, and the wall's a dark plaster ocean, her upset hopeless squinting up into ocean drowning wall plaster)

is the one I sneak take you not knowing. Without your OK. Then I even show the picture to other people, people stare at picture of you you know nothing about.

There we have a story. A story instead of friendship. A story, instead of being alive.

EXPLOIT (fiction)

Why's photograph of a steak more interesting than freehand sketch of cow? Because the steak's a true story. My doctor's name is Miss Nobel; she says I will not die. I was lying on the couch in her livingroom, my head was in her lap, when she first told me that. I had not yet gotten sick.

Her son stood far as he could away and still be in same room with us, he was staring into glass bubbling fish cage, ignoring our talking, asking questions about overfeeding fish death. Miss Nobel held her cool hand on my forehead, her face huge sideways above me, she said, doctor explaining symptom, that she didn't want me to move in with her. Not *not just yet.* Just not. "I don't trust you," and smiled quite well.

This was my occasion for *ultimatum;* I understood, though, unfortunately, her point. The boy began sprinkling lethal dose of brine shrimp; little angelfish jerked snapped. Thing lying in her lap, my face, which I thought I was keeping angel-blank, made her say "Oh Jim you'll live. It won't kill you."

This was one year ago. Since then I have

gotten her accidentally pregnant, and unaccidentally abandoned her. But that was built into our deal, I feel. Both understood we would carry on exploiting each other's bodies, my body good enough to mash against hers. Both understood something's wrong with *me*.

And now for that matter my body's dying, I think. "Opportunities present themselves" my doctor would say, "to these bacteria, they take advantage, never fail to take advantage of a situation they can move in and exploit."

Fear? she says. We're sitting in her office, on civilian unsterile chairs, I'm clothed up, not yet a nude lying on her papered steel butcher table.

Heart flutter? she says. Feeling of smothering, cardiac pain?

Worst at night, trying to sleep? Can't sleep, panic?

Yes. I admit. This humiliation now, is that a symptom?

Swallow, she says.

Miss Nobel leaves me sitting in her office, goes to leaf up science paper on Irritable Bowel Syndrome. She brought her kid to work today, he's *standing* on the steel table, seeking through his plastic Visible Man with organs showing all in different colors and its bland transcending futuristic face—kid staring, then probes with his fingertip and suddenly grabs himself at the indicated spot, thump, *here* my blue pancreas. Follows path downward till points at colon on plastic man and asks it "Then what?"

I explain, from across the room, that in this popularized toy model toymakers have hidden the connection between the colon and the asshole. Says, he's seven now, "What's the assholt?" just as his mother walks back in. An asshole, she says slowly, is a person who thinks he's more important than everybody else. He hurts the people around him. He is a guy who stinks.

Procedure for diagnosis, she says, is largely one of exclusion. We must determine you *do not* have one of the following:

> **an obstructing tumor**
> **coronary disease**
> **pulmonary tuberculosis**
> **perforation of the GI tract**
> **cancer of the esophagus**
> **renal disease**
> **stomach cancer** darling

She kisses me on front of the throat. We begin, she says, with stool samples.

Seven ways to be dying, is dying just a case of not getting my way? For my girlfriend, I spread my shit with wooden coffee-stick onto little slip cardboards: reveal my everyday life. Don't be shy, I love you but a doctor's impersonal, she sees your body as device. Your belief that you are about to die, even that we can consider only a symptom.

Yeah, of impending deadness.

Probably not, my entrail dove—and the

digestion very erratic? A lot of flatulence? All those strange eructations I was hearing last night? That means burps. Like a machinegun!

I can't stop burping. I can't sleep, burping, I have to take the pills to stop it. That's why I was acting so nasty when—

Hypnotics and, hey very interesting, a muscle relaxant. That was creative. Stop those. We will also X-ray and sonogram you. Because there are sometimes congenital malformations. You may have been born with the incorrect form.

My doctor, three diplomas Arkansas Pennsylvania New York hung like pictures on the seamless sheets of wall knotless oak, she in her office has only one hung actual picture: a painting: human being, flayed.

The painting's mounted on a roller blind. The man in it, I think he's the averaged-out science ghost of my doctor's ex-husband. Black needle points his TRACHEA (CARRIES AIR TO LUNGS), skull pale shaved gray he's side-turned not looking at us, each visible part explained in block letters. ESOPHAGUS (PASSES BETWEEN LUNGS TO STOMACH), leaning forward he's like in suspense, *Abduction of Vocal Cords for Breathing.* My doctor's ex-husband from Arkansas, father of her child, is roller-blind ripped open. His HYOID BONE and THYROID CARTILAGE pits and ridges exposed labelled with needle arrows from mouth gape down to his opened-out guts all within him visible.

He's looking *up*. To him something coming from above. He's open: but no heed for us staring at his works, us patients supposed to be amused by picture of somebody worse humiliated than us even: he's not open for us. On his roller blind stares undissected unlabelled eyes up into spring of the dowel works, his ruined body dreams what HAND may come to restore him, roll up his shame hidden again, balm stared-at guts with shroud peace. *Sensation of smothering.* Keep journal daily recording your symptoms, fold the journal pages, she says, over yourself, makes a mental carapace, see how often page by page you have not yet died.

Sensation enormous weight pressing.

Fear people can see through my clothes.

Fear people can see through my skin in inner processes.

Fear of impending punishment.

Non-wish to die on street, fear mockery, downtown Candyland bystanders kicking my body, brownshirt Candyland cops kicking my face, kicking, drill hole in my heels, pass wire through hang me up in center of town, punch stomach contents roar out mouth. Fear all this seen by all.

My doctor pokes long blue stick swab in back of my throat, it makes me gulp blank air, then she strokes that swab once across a slip of glass. Glass looks clean. She drips stain like blood, one drop, then makes a glass sandwich of that and puts it in the microscope.

I focus. It's focusing through depth; things,

the shapes, are atop each other, reaching down up into blur. The things. These things're in my throat; I try to clear throat, hiccup.

Inside my throat: red saltshaker-looking animals slide; I see outlines like a kid draws human as all outside crayon boundary. Inside the beasts is emptiness, just some slight clear-jerking life, nervous water. Animalcules slow twist and tumble by same locomotion your saltshaker floats through your kitchen at noon: not possible.

The microscope has two lights in, I switch off one. Now hollow-wall bugs are floating at cold sunset, throwing empty-frame shadows through each other, they look even eviller but at least evening-obscure, dim, dim's better. I turn wheel to make the slide pan to left; there I run into a *gang.* Some saltshaker things've connected each other up in long helix ladder snake. This ladder its own animal! Whole ladder whips back forth slowly, all individual beasts knowing how to cooperate, and they scorpion wrap around this one dark red quivering spot, which must be living innocent meat.

They've got it trapped. I can feel the spot in back of my throat where the swab hit. Switch off microscope light.

Extirpate. Sterilize. I watch till she wipes down microscope slide with cotton soaked in clean fatal clean alcohol.

Miss Nobel has a face that changes with changing light. I tell that to her in words, changing her face again: she puts her hand over my eyes tight, "then stop *looking*." Total blackness. "Do you want me when you can't see me?" Her voice without its animal—I reach out start taking her blouse off, trying to see collarbones with my fingers. Says "Keep your eyes shut—can you hear me through your stomach?" Puts her face to my stomach says *Beeeep...Soouund.* I say: I hear you. "Then you still have an appetite."

I love the picture of you in my mind, I say. She says, "That sounds sort of cold. What does a picture feel like?"

Miss Nobel, we're sitting facing into her strange green translucent-stone fireplace, cherry-wood mantel, old Korean porcelain stuff atop, all-orange sex languor red dark wine comfort and shared blindness of the fire. "If you ever want to betray me." Yes? I say. "If you decide—what do you mean *yes?*" "I love you. You're the last person I'd ever hurt." She sits looking in the fire: "Poison, I think. Love is blind...what can fake love see?"

Then her son home, sitting in the dining-room bashing the heads of two dolls together. I'm still swimeyed looking into the fire; Miss Nobel sitting against me, back to my back, facing into the diningroom. I can't see her. Can this way picture very clearly her back.

Us all eating dinner off white glaring china. Why (boy wants to know) do some things (looking at his mother) not go with other things (at me)? What goes with what?

Science taste tests me and him try: my red wine poured in bowl atop a clot of his peanutbutter, stirred into blood soup, then soberly by us both tasted: the peanutbutter, he states, lousy now; I note the red wine's not what it was. Yet (black pepper into peppermint icecream, borscht into orangejuice) what's created, we agree, is a *new food*, a new *bad* food, so it is not true (we become especially pedantic) that some things don't go together, no they *go* together but *should not*.

Unemployed me in Doctor Nobel's diningroom with Doctor Nobel's son. We are chopping Cocoa Krispies into cottage cheese, this is good! and she says "You gobble your food. Do you always gobble your food?"

According to Miss Nobel sometimes all these symptoms, terrifying symptoms, occur from mere overeating, especially in *infants*.

She's still at table, helping the kid do his homework, I'm lying in livingroom on sofa face down stuffed in the black crack.

I'm stuffed.

Can't swallow.

Math is everywhere, she's telling her child, he trying to sit upside-down in the chair, think how everything around you can be described mathematically. Kid looks suspiciously upside-down around him. The walls, she says, they all have measurements! The books and dishes and the carpet hairs and every single thing in this house was planned out by somebody, not by us, by people we don't even

9

know. They drew it on paper, figured it with numbers, before it was ever made. Kid puts hands over his eyes, then uncovers to stare up at her, he's upset. Was your face? he asks.

Our faces were made by BIOLOGY. What's upsetting you? Boy: I don't want all those people in here! They ruined everything, they touched everything! How come biology, who wrote biology? Cause biology, she says, works totally by mathematics: the cells of our bodies *multiply*. You were a cell in my belly, then you went two four eight sixteen. Look how our hands fit together left and right. We're made out of math.

He says: *No wait*. What about stuff I *do*? Like would if I kill somebody be mathematic? Wouldn't that get around the math?

They have different sciences to explain different things. I guess a murderer would be explained by psychology, or penology.

What's penology.

Prison, she says.

He says, *Prison* is science. OK, right. So I know what, he says: so if I rob a bank, it's cause I want to ADD to my money. That's math it's legal! And then I murder off all the scientists, cause they're all crazy numbers, I'm learning how to SUBTRACT.

On sofa. Scared. Like stone at base of throat. Cannot gulp.

Breath squeezed dizzy sucking narrow air on her sofa with her boy sitting next to me playing with two dolls. Dolls golden plastic vision in my dark-float-spot eyes, the two dolls standing on my chest are thousand feet tall, dolls last thing I saw before passout coma and death, grief eternal retina ghost-photo of two plastic girl dolls.

The blonde doll, Skipper, is telling the redhead Ko-Boo-Tah Piggy, "You're *fat!* Fat means you die young! Ko-Boo-Tah Piggy is a dead *fat-soh.*" Ko-Boo-Tah Piggy reply squeak parody voice "Only a *terrible creep* would say such a thing, you're a CREEP. CREEP." Piggy furious scream squeaking CREEP! and Skipper starts answering *Not a* calmer, in almost the boy's own voice: *Not a/*CREEP! *Not a/* CREEP!

Skipper doll and Ko-Boo-Tah Piggy doll play I AM NOT A ROCK. Skipper stands on my fore-head, her little high heels steady acupuncture. Ko-Boo-Tah Piggy hovers in the air above me, above Skipper, just floats acting deaf and blind. Skipper launches insult jokes from my forehead, tries to make the floating doll scream or laugh. Tries to make her react *say* something. But Piggy contains herself. I stare up at indomitable Ko-Boo-Tah, how does she do it? Piggy impermeable as plastic, un-changing doll stone island in the sky. Skipper mere human can't be heard, her voice gets desperate but she's all voice, all talk air nothing, she might as well try to reach the not-yet-born.

I'm sitting up finally OK edge of the sofa, me and the boy play scissors paper rock. It's late for him; Miss Nobel wants him to sleep. In our game me and him both want to be paper. Keep doing that, one—two—*paper* we make two sheets paper open hands just look flat at each other.

I'm supposed to sleep.

Night has fallen. Night every direction.

In the bed of Miss Nobel I lie alone awake. My burping, gulping air, farts, turning over groaning, whisper questions "death a *gut feeling?* feel it *in my bones?*" these've forced my girlfriend doctor to go sleep in her son's room. I follow find her lying balanced edge of her son's narrow bed, she says "I don't want to wear out on you," her blue robe arms cover her face block her ears, I beg her to come back, I can't sleep alone. "Disgust isn't hate," she mumbles exhausted. "But I used to hate the cadavers they'd put us onto. I hated them *as people.* I don't want to sniff your cheek...formaldehyde."

No sleep at all. Followed by oatmeal.

Kid eating Honeycomb Cereal. We're alone, his mother's still in the shower. Ko-Boo-Tah Piggy and Skipper are sleepily still bickering. Skipper is eating a peanut, in the shell. "Stop ignoring me," says Ko-Boo-Tah Piggy. Skipper mutters "You don't exist," trying to eat the bigger-than-her-head peanut. Ko-Boo-Tah Piggy picks up the enormous sugar dispenser, flies into the air and bombs sugar into boy's orangejuice. The boy tells her, in his own voice, "now you're just calling attention to yourself."

We all agree to ignore Ko-Boo-Tah Piggy. I can't eat this stunned rubber oatmeal. I push at it. Spread it around the inside bowl, bodying every sight of china bone. A few seconds from now I will start to suffocate. That I know because I hear the dolls' arguments as from down inside huge garbage pail. I'm sweating breakfast sweat. Shove and bounce spoon off oatmeal, "I'm *chewing*," I say, mashing it over rim of bowl mashing spillover into the table, talking out loud makes a breath of voice bridge sound to distract dying, "chewing is *natural*. After you *eat anything*, it looks *about like this*," mottled gristle clumps.

Doctor Nobel's pushing through, late for clinic: Stopping past the lab on my way, I need your samples. Right at table she pricks my finger blood drip, has me drool saliva up a little tube, hands me urine cup, "are you sweating? good," presses my upper lip with a microscope slide.

I walk the boy to school, then head alone slow through Candyland back toward my apartment. Stainless-steel diner Boethius Eatery. Reddening diabolical polaroids taped in the window. Must squint to see these photos are meat plates. My eyes seeing this food so distant abstracted lead my stomach inside, my eyes seek the menu language words to place the order and eyes receive the moonbeige plate lunch chop of lamb. Don't *gobble*. Wait. Wait for peace. Other plates for other patrons fly above my head. Trying to see their plates as peaceful moons, I only see plate paths, orbits of dry air. How would you photograph an invisible moon?

I cut into the lamb. Supposed to eat with calm with no haste. Peace, achieve it. Medley Mix

Vegetable beside lamb is green-gray and orange-gray. Chewing is this natural process. Slowly, without gulp. But my trachea says spasm No it's too soon.

So, slowly. So slowly I slow cut all the chop into lamb, little, squares. Then, I landscape spread a platewide valley bed of Medley. And dot this, dot by dot, with lamb cubes in astrologic math symmetry. The food's placid now, cold too, more abstract. Maybe I'm little hungry.

I wait.

They've made the dark pocket-diner seem bigger by coating the ceiling in mirror. What you see when you stare up: yourself inverted above yourself: a wrong point of view.

The mirror says it's true story. Light hitting makes verification. True story is more interesting. How long after the light hits do you become interesting? Does being interesting answer any of your questions?

I have killed this lamb. Should I order dessert?

Do not attempt EAT till you achieve the peace of the belly! I tell the Greek man I'm not ready yet!

I cut lamb shred smaller, smash it all around Eden medley. Lamb was living in peace till I ordered it dead so I could EAT gulp and turn it to shit.

A true story's still only a story. I can't and won't eat this. Time to pay *damages*, take a constitutional.

Every billboard has a back side. The twenty-foot strawberry photo billboard shortcake is fresh and almost makes me hungry, red-white beauty you'd really like to rip into. Walk past, then turn to see the back:

no it's all black.

Bigger billboard, a bigger story's truer. Thirty-foot red dinnerplate: little truck-tire-size sushi cross-sections in rows two by three. Folds of salmon ginger in a separate moment. Green crumble of *wasabe*, addressing the ginger. Spray of squared grass. Beauty order killing a degree of appetite. Desire to look, never to chaos eat. And walk past, behind billboard turn:

close stare of Japanese eyes, thirty-foot slice of eye face. Selling Fuji film by staring. *What we have seen*

Am I going to die.

I want answers. [i-am-going-to-die] no I mean, I mean I want to be the man up in the window, man who sees. Who looks down.

There's light behind me. I belong here. Night I'm indoors, a shadow. At home.

Because I live above a restaurant there will be homeless guy outside, sorting through our iron dumpster.

Because about where I live, I know things.

Backside of the restaurant sits iron boatsize
dumpster. Half-boat of food garbage every night,
barge swamping in salad sea.

One dark tube-shape man in dumpster.
Squats on hill of shredded cabbage excelsior.

He holds cold cooked green potato up to the
moonlight.

Is this piece of garbage a piece of food?

The man in the window, who's not homeless, me, has all the answers. *Yes.*

Is it good to eat?

Eat and find out.

What if it makes me sick?

OK sniff it first.

Smells like. Like, moonlight.

Sounds pretty. Take a bite, Bo.

Could be rancid.

*Bite so I can watch what
happens.*

Does somebody got to eat everything?

I love a story. Eat up.

If I don't eat this, who will?

*There's other tramps less
philosophic than you.*

Let him have it then.

*Don't be throwing away good
food! Just put your mouth on it. Or I'll rush out there
and tell you leave our garbage property alone.*

Salad man eats potato slowly, his face down,
because I'm the man in the window I have the
answers and he doesn't. But he doesn't change, a

story is about change, I mean about crime, how crime always changes a thing. Looks up at the moon with his face still hungry.

He's going away. Wish he wouldn't.

I don't know.

Isn't moonlight becoming to this courtyard rubble?

I don't have answers. Stomach spasm. Squatting at window, pressure upward ass gut clench *hold out*, sweat and looking at moon piles of yard junk layers throwaway.

I think all this stuff was gutted out of this building. They broke out walls of old apartments, threw all the evicted stuff out in yard.

Yard rotting plaster hunks darked out with soak of old restaurant slop overflow, that moonpale leg-shape underneath is a stack of written-on legal pads, thousands of pages strapped with rusty wire into puffy stuck-together whitened bundles. *Thousands of pages* all written on in black felt pen now soaked-away soft purple thick by old rain, not one word is readable.

Four old apartment lives turned into two sprawl new *units*. Two *modern units* with real tenants. Whose valuables are not garbage but property. Then there's me. *Squat* would be called an abandoned apartment but this where I live isn't even that. It's just inbetween space, extra, waste room.

We don't even know who we evicted. Out there is ten shoeboxes stacked lids crushed out at corners, dirt frosting and a few potato bugs. Each box holding its single clump of water-stuck-together snapshots, snapshots fused size and weight of a little pot-roast. If you try to recover one picture slice it unpeels itself blank paper. The outer surface of each clump where not bugeaten shows little hands, foreheads.

I found blowing across yard one old black & white polaroid Thanksgiving turkey eaten carcass on a table, and way in background flashbulb black there's a sideways screaming little girl floating. Put that on my wall.

Evicted four apartments worth of humans on this second floor like discard rubble was banquet to serve mouth courtyard. Owner ripped walls add rooms to surplus luxury rooms, each new enormous present-day tenant two bed two bath *two living-rooms*. But even they didn't want two kitchens each. So why rip out old plumbing, true luxury says just wall off waste part of floor. Two abandoned kitchens connect up by long narrow slot between new walls, and that's my house, two dark old kitchens.

No exit door, crawl in out window. No bathroom, down fire escape backyard I dug latrine hole roofed it rust Chevrolet hood, hung outhouse curtain I strung of buttoned strings. Old buttons found everyplace in courtyard. If buttonhole still shred of fabric thread, one pluck and rot fastening plucks out. Behind curtain buttons I sit at latrine gut discussion. The churchbells next door to mark off excruciations. Hours where it's not worth climbing back my upstairs hole, churchbells begin to sound constant. I'm going to die this way bells.

I shouldn't eat. I open big cardboard box, ten pounds scallops butter cream sauce, I say *I really shouldn't*. The building owner wants me to eat. *I really shouldn't take this*. Owner lives in unit next to me, is old Chef runs restaurant downstairs. All day I breathe soak in food cooksmell. Chef a great chef really knows how to addict the nose into brain needing adoring food. Then midnight he sends a kid up my fire escape balancing me huge box of the leftovers.

I eat, never cook. Two stoves and a mattress. I don't have a child or fishtank or cactus plant or any living thing.

I have pictures on walls. Layers of pictures:

old texturized thriftstore oilpainting of Faust looking at bubbling crucible,

and a bookplate histrionic Oedipus bloodeyed black&white blind trying to *stare*,

and the newspaper death Jerzy Kosinski with baggie over his head,

and picture of man signing contract, he's photographer famous for those My Lai photos,

young Albert Speer laughing in dark holding a flashlight beam straight up at his face,

hand-colored soft calendar scene John Rockefeller kneeling beside a toy train,

lurid big opera poster of Wozzeck holding knife starved-looking,

magazine rip-outs Le Petomaine and Oppenheimer and Ludwig II, there's lots more, too much, smothering now the ceiling too. I put new ones every day, whatever I find—use tape put layer over layer, now whole thing sags away from the walls like a quilt.

Buttons curtain in wind outside little chickling click sounds. They're making gravy air below me. If I breathe: stomach-roommate wake and gasp. No breathe. Not chime bells.

Downstairs the restaurant kitchen. The people who do things. Fat man, that is fat Albion the son of Chef owner, fat and full beard pale Albion steps over a low comb of chicken wire into small white room. He's wearing big nipples-to-knees apron blood-blotched and blood-wiped painter smock earthtone. Holding snapshot camera, the name of this plastic camera GRAB & GO. In his other hand a long knife.

The turkey runs around its cage room in stupid small attacks on each corner, gogging. Makes huge pale man with camera and knife laugh, idiocy funny, he kneels down laughing. Then he does two things: makes a sudden cut-short yell, UUT: fat bird feathers and stops, looking right at him: Albion *flashes* the camera in its eyes. Bird, beak open, staring, runs straight at him mute, runs its neck right into his held-still knife.

Chef his father gray skinny strong old man called Chef like Maestro, watching from the kitchen. *Olé* he yells. Raises a cleaver and brings it down again. The breast in Chef's grip's sundered from its neck. Necks in one pile, they look alike, beige food-pipes, food.

Beyond Chef a big Greek woman chopping a hundred yellow onions fast one by one, woman who consumes only meat and tobacco, hating vegetables kills them all. Skins of dead onions go in a big plastic can, meat of dead onions into big steel bucket. Knife chopping against a slab of oak tree, also dead. Oak taking on brown onion-acid slashmarks.

Photo behind chopping woman calendar advertising a brand of knife by posing an orange girl in primary-blue bikini, she holding up huge chromium cleaver like hand mirror. Beach scene ignored by the cigarette-sucking knife woman with large shoulders, who lives walled between hung pots on iron loops and sack sandbags undemolished onions.

Murder is against the laws of man.

Cats are fascinating.	Cows are boring.
Dogs are loyal.	Pigs are boring.
Horses are smart.	Chickens are boring.
Parrots can talk.	Sheep are boring.

Eye of dead fish. *Because a fish can't even purr*. Eye black circle on scummed white circle. Dead centered motionless staring up.

The restaurant places each table within its own zone of black calm. All it takes to do that is light.

My doctor's diningroom has chinese rug edges exactly one foot from all four oak wall baseboards.

In the restaurant kitchen the fish eye looks

180 degrees. Fish in death sees grease, fastwalking men, falling plate, slops, cigarette butt, glare light, and the diningroom door source of steady-arriving garbage.

I can burn/cook fish stick in broiler then dump on a plate, fish skin dry crinkled silver black, ugly good-tasting blindman gnaw. However this is *presented* visual restaurant fish painted with herb butter wet of wet flesh, brought ashore on *bed* of kale like fish chose to nap here, festooned almonds hazelnuts in chip, *festooned* means artful scatter chaos for edibility of beauty, just eat, we already stirred this up you won't be making a mess, dig in.

Out front of the restaurant there's an awning single peachcolored motion. Behind the restaurant, rubble as noted. Has not organized itself during one evening.

Albion sitting on dining area floor, bang bang bang both hands openhanded pounding the screaming vacuum canister.

After closing. Lights up bright no more mystery table dim zones.

Chef comes out of kitchen sits beside his son on rug.

"I'm sorry" yells Chef over vacuum. "I was busy. I was painting." Rubs the fat shoulder of his son. "I was sketching my old street in Milano. And I drew a woman on the sidewalk. There was my house behind her. And I can't draw. Too flat the house, it looked like a table she was lying on. It felt I was drawing crazy. Did not understand a hairy woman on a table. Drawing crazy. At once I remember your *dinner party*. And I said: Not now. Too sad. I can't go to dinner where there's no food at it."

"The dinner is a *performance*. Like a play. You eat first, then you come see what your son does with his life."

Vacuum roar for two minutes.

"You used to be skinny little kid. Used to eat anything you want."

"*You're* still skinny. *You* eat any damn junk."

Chef slaps his own belly, not smiling. "My cooking is good. And my paintings are no good, I know. Terrible. But I can dish out what I make. So I'm not supposed to be alive, but I'm alive."

Albion falls over on the melodrama vacuum hugging it teddybear roaring, he roars "I'm addicted to food!"

"But I never see you eat nothing! When do you eat?"

"I'm *glad* you didn't show up! I stunk! I found out I wasn't ready! It was really just a crummy bunch of questions."

"You serve people questions for dinner, huh. You know what the special tonight was? You missed it. Veal in raspberries. Turn off the vacuum!"

"Oh. And you *made it work*, right?"

"I know—finally figured it out—cook raspberries in savory. That was the answer."

"Question!" Albion says. "Why not—"

Vacuum roar pause. Albion hugging machine says Ummm. "Why not have CUISINE where things *don't* go together? So people can see the *problem* of food. So they learn what's veal and what's raspberries."

"Not understand you!" Chef grabs long cord, yank, vacuum moans stop. Albion can't let go of dead machine. Chef low murmur voice "I poisoned a table once. Nobody died. The owner reacted how you would hope. I had led him to imagine I knew how to pick mushrooms. I did not forget that ever. That was my first job in Rome.

"People want to enjoy their meal. *I* want to. A man sit peaceful in beautiful room, and have these surprises brought in, *special*, all inventions he never dream to taste, he says *god jesus I love this thing.*"

"They're all fat pigs who come in here. Rich assholes deserve to starve."

"*Hey* fatboy." Chef stands up. "Vacuum up my damn rug."

Two in the morning them yelling, arguing, shoving each other, that's them I hear coming upstairs. They go in their apartment, fight keeps up scream "we gave you life! Me and your whore mother! What's so terrible? Why your life isn't good enough *performance?*"

Bumpbumpbump from the other apartment, other side of my hole. The great writer lives there, him I've never seen. I guess he doesn't get out much. Just hear him keyboard click. Trying now to write or sleep, so he yells in thuds.

Son "You wasted your whole life! You just work for the EATERS! You forgot what it means to be a CHEF!" That's when the Chef and Albion crashing starts, metal pots thrown, next noise amazing maybe floor-to-ceiling bookcase getting pulled down on top of a human being. See, now great writer stopped banging on the wall. Instead I hear him listening.

Chef and son gone to their separate bedrooms. Kitchen they share is empty. Scorched. Wide black burns across kitchen walls, puncture holes in refrigerator door, oven shattered into black and white metal sections spilling across floor. Cabinets wrenched and shelves pried away. Splatter red paint and blue everyplace, worst on countertop like paint exploded there where a cook might chop onions and weep.

On their kitchen table a cherry tart sitting out on a plate. All night it sits, a blue light blinking on it.

Downstairs the restrooms are dark. They were designed by Chef. Fresh basket of dirty mushrooms on rude wood table, brush dried flowers, French-country-kitchen enamel bowl and pitcher. Iron fireplace, oak sinks oak partitions, brass plumb fittings, heated towel racks real towels carved soap. Breughel print showing in mirror, so the eater in mirror sees himself in the painting, a dancer in the warm foreground.

Father allowed son try designing restrooms.

Remained on paper: son wanted a stainless-steel counter in the center, white tile all around, hospital operating theatre overhead lights, all fixtures fixed for wheelchair grapple, and tall bright mirrors at a backward slant to make eater's face a no-chin weasel, eater's body below it a blobbing expanse of draperied fat.

In his room middle of the night the naked Albion's lined up glass flask of dietary fiber, brown glass jar vitamins, carafe of filtered water.

He takes a potato, puts it on small steel anvil, sledgehammer thuds it repeated till flat broken.

His ashtray full of butts, and air yellow smoke. The corner a factory with cigarettes slit lengthwise, tobaccos blended on a board, a pestle, bits of caffeine pills.

He takes a pinch of fiber into his mouth— one vitamin—one sip of water to wash down.

East wall is all diet and theatre books; south wall all chemical and engineering. And a wall chart:

STYROID   CRYSTAL   CELLULAR   GRAINED
STRENGTH . . . . ➔ . . . . INSIPIDITY
SOUR   BITTER   SALTY   SWEET

Swabs potato juice off the anvil with pieces of flat potato, and drops all potato bits into metal well of an electric machine. Seals the well, shuts lid switches on. The centrifuge noise crunches whines like whole-mammal liquefier. He lights a cigarette.

In the noise he can think; he can talk softly.

"The food goes in, it comes out shit. Why live?"

Can't hear himself so OK.

"Equality between flavors, chance operations to pick meal elements—*eliminate desire.*

"*Eliminate hunger:* create food with no desirability. Slight perpetual nausea. You think you're some saint? You *caused* your girlfriend to *die.* Why not just stop eating? *She has.* Why not stop shitting? *She has.* Why not disappear if all you do is exist—A COOK'S GOTTA CREATE, ARTIST GOTTA EAT—if all you do is *damage*, making more recipes for waste culture fragment artifact pollution turds, if all you do is *shit on your father and shit on the people you love?*"

Belt slips within the machine, shrieks smoke burning rubber—he hugs it to stop centrifugal rubber smoke scream then clomps naked coughing out through battle kitchen yelling, yelling to rescue his father—"EVACUATE!"

Chef grinding veal, his son carries in his arms human-torso-size red meat wrapped in loose-weave cloth, drops it on table. Huge knife balances easy in son's fat hand. Asks his father should I remove the netting? or strike with the knife through it?

Line drawing curve tube. Fat finger funnels along tube slowly; woman salesman's saying "this is where the cattle arrive at the killing hammer. And you see this little detail of a curved path we created just for their sake—so they won't know the hammer's coming. For the uh, for purpose of being humane. They never realize what it's all been about, they don't die in fear. Plus you know some people feel the meat tastes better that way."

Face of Chef big, his squint down close to a sheet of veal eyeing the marbling. "This meat for the shredder," and lifts the dead muscle sheet feeds it to a cast-aluminum mouth. "Observe my respect for dignity of cow. How polite I handle *chunk*. So nobody get mad at me today.

"Nobody want to bleed like me. Nobody want to put themselves *in* the food! I, an old man, I sweat like a pig every day! We are here to serve the meal—to *serve the meal*, we working for the meal, we got to be ingredients, us! Like this shredder [slaps its grrr-ing metal belly], you *use* it. Takes a soul to use well, to use for beauty. This is *heavy-duty* shredder. Enjoys to be used. It don't betray me ever—I hit it, still it works good. Gives itself. Last for years. When finally breaks, I'll sell it to the Junkyard King. We are employees of our customers, employees go *into* the meal."

The veal bright pile of red clay. Around it, worker man scrapes wood cuttingboard, mute, worker woman carries bucket vegetables to sink, mute, they don't look at Chef.

"Every week I have to fire a kid for some *thing*, is very hard. Them, they have no worries like me, they don't care about the food, they have no ideas. Come and go. I don't know who they are. Not one of them seems like cares a damn. That why I get my own restaurant now, before some owner decide I'm too old, throw me out. Now I can fire whoever won't *suffer to work*, and nobody can't fire me. I'm a *heavy-duty!*"

A whitesmocked kid risking his pale right hand inside an iron appliance to pluck out with fingertips from wicked blades a jamming radish. He shouts "Nobody is watching! I could steal this radish!" Two other kitchen workers drop their knives grab him, struggling drag him to back door and shove him out trips falls in the courtyard rubble. Door slam and he's alone with the back of building like shut church, he's shouting "It's my fault! I've hurt everyone I ever loved!"

Door opens, in unison they yell "Get lost, asshole!"

"I am the waste! You are the flavor! You have to survive but I don't!"

"Go *home*, shithead!" slam.

Serving platter of lamb in shank, the greens

are mint, pasta hair of angel, around it the flesh of candlelight, off-focus kiss of wineglass, and up the wall huge walnut slab with the head of a little duck, just tiny head black mounted there and yellow bill, black little eyes.

Fired salad-maker's shouting "*Home? Home?!*"

Wedged in a steel closet booth, a security guard squints at his little black & white monitor: tiny image of the freed worker wandering off in back of the courtyard, kneeling in rubble mulch to hand-dig himself a home. Guard, eating cheeseburger, snorts once and flips the dial. A housewife screams delight on the gray little screen, then a glass drainpipe's releasing cataract of clean fresh water down into a place nobody in the world can see, a place below bottom of TV.

Potato eye. Potato eye wouldn't hurt any-body to eat. It's not disease, the eye, but's ugly. Nobody hungry for it. Potato eye gouged with metal tool out of its potato, flipped in the bottom of a plastic barrel. Thousands other eyes follow with peelings even whole eye-sprouting potato rejects, till the barrel's dirty beige full.

Whole barrel one motion lifted dumped into big square hole in the wall, plywood door shut bang.

Eyes fall in the dark, turning.

Eyes land underground in basement steel bin on wheels.

Bin on a railroad track, slow rolls down the track a few feet. Chef restaurant plan big dining floors underground, expanding outward downward, workers basement digging dirt hauling like mining operation. Workers dirt-colored naked to waist pushing wooden wagons of dirt laughing arguing:

"Aw man, it's not enough to *act* like you're good!"

"Course it is! Who cares what you *feel* like? Go ahead *feel* like killing people, as long as you don't do it!"

Throws a fistful of dirt at his friend, "If I *want* to kill you then I'm a killer pig and I don't deserve your friendship!"

His friend throws dirt more back harder, "If you *wanna* kill me but you *don't* I could really respect you for that!"

"*Goddamn* it Robbie—*ask me why I want to kill you!*"

Flurry of dirt.

Couple dogs start barking at them.

A dozen fatbelly black dogs mope through construction dig. On back of one dog hangs a rat, yellow eyes. Dog and rat lie there looking at a bone, dog never bothering bury it. Another dog steals runs bone a few paces, drops it, forgets.

One skinny poodle caught here too—filthy never eats, bites at its own paws. Rolling on back biting paws bloody, legs and flanks dirt blood.

Most of the fat black dogs lie in the dirt howling. Each deep in own throat like howling to self.

A worker scoops bin of potato eyes, starts

throwing eyes to the dogs. Dogs don't care about potatoes. The peels and eyes cover them like stuck ash.

Old worker in overalls starts wide iron rake reap the potato peels together with paper and coffee grounds from a previous offering. Howling dogs stand, shake off potato, hop over rake, circle once and lie down back in fresh-rake dirt, not ceasing howl.

Worker old man rakes up dirt-potato garbage pile drifts beside the river.

River because rusty big pipe sticking out of restaurant down, flood roars out pipe aimed straight down at earth, flood brown dug itself out a hole dirt-deep lake then boiling up rush brown scary foam ripping a riverbank all down slant of dig against the ancient stone foundation wall down alongside diagonal earth-entering tunnel the men are digging, waste river roars off into that outer black. Sends back hollow thrum through filth-wetted old wall, echo like huge ceramic, like river feeds enormous not-filling jar.

Worker rakes the potatoes on into the river.

All-naked muckcoated worker skinny body strong muck arms, wields a long pole, on end pole basket dips into the river, he muscles muckbasket up and into a mining sieve so drip recovered muck back down on foam roar. Another worker picks up the tray of drippedout muck, bangs it twice expert then slams upsidedown on a wood picnic-table, makes long rectangle cake of filth. Twelve workers at table chop with long thin knives delicately at this cake. Choppers faces worn tired, mouths steady twist distaste keep blades chop seeking.

Big triangle bell gongs slow lunch. All other workers sit down, open lunchboxes, but not these twelve at the table. They stop their chopping and just sit looking at the earth.

"Not hungry. No," when you ask one of the men, "mostly never do find nothing good. And it takes a tough stomach. See Barbara down there. She says her cousin found a diamond one time, that's what keeps some of the younger kids at this job—maybe find something, gold filling or like a real pearl. So Chef'll give 'em nice bonus. I guess I don't think that way no more." All the time clutching at his stomach.

Out my window what I watch, rubble yard and beyond that the buildings, the church source of chime and next door library. Carved into City of Candyland Free Library building, hundreds of little separate windows; a reader in each, each sitting still looking down eating with eyes a book.

Library when I go inside scares me too much to read. Books in thousands like food that never gets thrown out, I go instead sit by magazine rack. Magazines are at least disappearing fast as they appear. At least have pictures. Here's a picture of white china food-plate.

Plate white because no ink there on the magazine back. When they put nothing on the page that gets you to look. No ink makes white halo around a single all glow potato, they made it out of light one spotlight for roundness two spotlights for glisten, white golden potato meat broken baked ideal midday midwest white, full weight and hot of potato, unstinting crisp vellum skin, twice the potato size of life sour cream glaciating across butter slicks into pleasure food crevice. The magazine people promise. They want to feed me, love me, help. They promise they'll answer questions. Across the top says EAT LIGHT.

Librarian foxfaced skinny lady with white hair one long white glove draped over one shoulder, she suggests try dewey decimal ethics 170, medical self-help 610, try Finnish legends Kalevala, maybe coroner's reports on murdered farmgirls, check jailer's questionnaires criminals Latvian prison system, electromicrographs jagged-edge eyelash, cello sonata depicting suicide under influence of a large mirror—she's sitting talking louder and louder, thumping her little desk, "other cultures, a *banquet!* the experience of the collective like a clogged grate, endless *food for thought* how to live what to do, *every possible opinion every possible error!*"

Escape to a book-wall corridor maze, dark. Wander to where short lady and her same-height son standing, he has a book in hand and he's talking soft about it, looks at the book but speaks his own words, speaks passion and speaks, finally his mother seeks among what's walled them in the size book she wants, pulls it from shelf, beats to shush, once and twice, with her book the top of his head.

Green stairs lead up to medical library, where I mainly came in here to get to. But'm frozen gaping at the obese man who got there first, *filling* the top of the stairs holding open a red book written to his size, yardwide covers and as I stare the man slips, falls to sitting down then starts very slow sliding down the steps, toward me, sliding sitting feet-first, silent this is a library, pantlegs curtain rise his dough calfs, obese face turned high and away from his experience, mouth prunes to each step by step bounce, and arms he might use to stop himself are instead hugging the red book, if he saves the book the book's going to save him, all the way down.

He's sitting hot right on my feet. "Don't go up there," he gasps.

Escape again, now to dimmest maze where no readers go, get myself lost alone in walls of books with no subject, scads of—*novels* these are I guess. No end to them. Randomly reach out for a book; worn-out it folds open like broken elbow. Looking at white paper with licorice markings...can't remember what this was for...move book close to face...sniff... lick a page once...it's dry: I don't get it. Lick again: lightly test my stomach with fingertips.

Windows of Blended Interfaith Church of Candyland next door stained glass dull blue colors never tell a story. Any hour I go in at least a few people are kneeling trying to launch prayers. Sound silent air organ pipes no music passing through and the prayer whisper hisses. Hear a word *poison*, sss again *poison*, that's not Latin. Black-ribbon-around-her-forehead woman holds pale hands over both eyes because that's praying when there's real poison in your body,

> "...pit of my stomach
> ...why Lord
> ...is the pit deeper than the mind
> ...throne of misery
> ...do You dwell there
> ...did You make the pit
> ...did You make the poisoner..."

across the aisle bony rat-girl eyes staring aloft punching the pew-back berating Jesus by name,

> "You gave me life in a candy store,
> made sure I got conceived there,
> You filled my parents with lust,
> set them fucking behind the counter,
> Then You waited. Made me fall in love with

my father,

> You showed me his candy-true eyes,
> how they turn fear into made-up marsh-

mallow,

> this was Your brilliant idea to have me

poison my mom OK and I did, but now You're not telling me how to get away with it! You *want* me to get caught? *Has that always been Your idea?*"

> Stay home safe. Safe caution is amber light.

In a few feet of sink counterspace I made a kitchen factory for pictures. Old sheetmetal enlarger, some plastic trays to receive prints for develop. Safelight light makes kitchen float amber on black shadow. Exposed paper blank looks dazzling amber. Slide it under developer surface night-drowning. Paper in developer so wet makes you thirsty, you want to drink it by trayful. Joggle the print, important to maintain agitation, "furious" means energy staring waiting rectangle of blank.

In one minute fade up shiny BLACK expanse surround and black bits in the white amber-staying center oval, the solid bit shadows inside oval create friend Dinah, that good friend I really know, whose side I'm on, never to betray, Dinah staring her beautiful because not-easily-hurt eyes at *viewer*, she's slightly scaring *viewer* but I've got her under my toxic liquid. It's OK developed, jerk her out dripping into tray *stop bath* make it stop drown vinegar smell into her nose sharp into eyes Easter egg her face. Yank and flip facedown in tray of fixer. So in another minute no activity, no more sensitive activity, I am safe to treat photo how my heart wishes. Switch on kitchen white light, blast it will have no effect because the face of my good friend is fixed.

A moth dinks against bare bulb. I hear same moment some rustle rat behind black-felt curtain, the kitchen opposite, my roommate a rat jolt noise whispers in noise rasp *"what* is the *matter* with you?" Moth rat-confederate draws a complicated sign around the light, a double-infinity with whorl, this insect signing its name, and slamming the bulb moth burns out. Flips in two arcs down where in a human kitchen it would have met a counter. There to rest all night. Humans are fair in dealings with moths. It could have laughed flittered its wings, "*what* is the matter with me?" could have recovered slowly in the smell of a lettuce shred and looked planningly at my window moon. But not a human kitchen, no moon in a darkroom, so where moth landed was in the developer tray. Blinded, then poisoned, then drowned. White wings out float the body in the green tray.

I didn't see that happen. Slide in next print then. Suddenly amber wings throw shadow down on my clean glossy paper.

Fuck all things that upset me. That's a contaminant. It died little bastard scared me. Use it. In arts we take up serendipitous accidental deaths of others, I make of moth corpse a developersoaked brush. It would wish me to use it I pretend. Hope when I'm dead some good artist sops my body in paint smashes it into his canvas, I pretend. Using moth as soppy splat onto unmade print of face, photograms of a moth-attacked Dinah result, flap wing bug nightmares to weak my photographed strong-eyed friend, that's redemption when something dead gets thrown at your feet, make negative to profit, corpse turn to account.

Treat all prints with clearing agent wash and dry according archival principles. This way the prints whether any good or not will last five hundred years. Dinah and me five hundred years locked by the eyes. A picture they'd be staring at next millennium if it were that good, those unborn wonder about subject and photographer and moth white ick wings between them, what *story* they'd wonder. And wish to touch us.

Outside beside slagheap's a recycling bin. Don't bin for re-use such organic garbage as an immortal moth.

On my kitchen floor, slide projector. This so it can shine onto the refrigerator white screen. I went to library checked out library slides ART, I'm trying to learn something.

First the kitchen is black. Then light tunnel glows click into a five-hundred-year-old drawing. You can do this now with a kitchen.

Fat arm of child. The fat children drawing five hundred years ago are naked. Fat arm sticks out through mouth of horrible mask. Fat live under dead tree. Vulture in tree five hundred years ago fat-eating vulture. Two children wear these masks: horrifying because masks of cruel old men. The two fat scaring on purpose with masks two other, unmasked children. One *good child* fallen in dirt while trying to run away. Center evil child *sticking his own fat arm through open mouth of mask.* He is cruel old man with his baby arm coming out his mouth.

Click *out* of jumps me five hundred years to now. All now is is my own kitchen in the dark me alone, terrible. Bleak school still waiting blackboard trying to learn.

New click opens five hundred years again. Trying to learn how they five hundred years ago drew idea: Allegory. Allegory now waste, nobody anymore can use it, it's in rubble section of library art. Because allegorical refrigerator no use to the starving. (I am dying...say. Can I get justice now, or do I have to wait five hundred years? Will if I can blame somebody else for me dead, help? Is a blast of white light death better? What practical use to be "immortal"? Who is it who is immortal for loyalty: Fido.) This drawing of Woman-dogs, antique Woman-dogs on my refrigerator. Women with dog-legs three legs each only, one in front two in hind, and woman breasts, wings of angels or is it griffins. They are like cast-iron beasts to prop steady a huge ball, because ball's unstable, upon it sits uneasily the naked great FAT WOMAN. The drawing has a name "Allegory of the Fall of Ignorant Humanity," so these women equal horror fears of the viewer's, I can't figure out the dog women but naked fat woman has a little label *Ignorance*. And Ignorance is propped up behind by skinny hungry witch naked *Avarice*, avarice could feel like you've got a tape-worm. Also helping prop's *beautiful* woman *healthy* naked ribboned with elaborated flow blindfold, who is she? She's gorgeous eternal, can we get her name?

Is she Love-Is-Blind? Is she Justice-For-Me? Her name, Jim, is INGRATITUDE.

My slide projector lives on the floor. Click and these horrible women are plastic-sucked back up into carousel dark machine. Nothing shining on my refrigerator door. Machine squats whirring like girl's little toy oven lightbulb inside ready to bake a toy cake feed me tiny. Out squint-thin cracks in slide projector where cheap plastic joins cheapest, intense light leaks. Cheap mistakes light up my kitchen walls with ghost point-finger needles and arrows.

Then I don't hear it click, though here in my hand is the clicker. Judge glares down on me. I myself checked him out of graveyard library, I brought him here clicked him here. Bloodshot-eye 15th century Cardinal. He's indignant how his flesh has to touch my refrigerator door. His fat stone head, circles carved under see-everything no-blink eyes by knife of self-guzzling years red wine. Lips compressed *shame*, not up to God does he look, it's not *his* shame, he's judge, he looks at *me*, looking *down*. I will not shiver. Jam my stare into his. Clamp to myself fierce, cleave clasp my century, yeh fuckyou deadman, oh god hey I'M STARVING

yank open door of the fridge and judge's head's blasted away in cold light blare white plastic vault, burning still-life fills my eyes: red ropes licorice! 3-D blocks white broken chocolate! I'm still blinking, not much real food here huh, and see a box of cookies same moment as realize the back refrigerator wall's still gesso plaster pale wash of that still-shining pastel CARDINAL FACE I swing around kick whirring projector across kitchen floor *because I'm hungry*, COOKIES cookies chocolate cookies. Cookies are little chocolate pictures stamped with woodcut of a schoolboy, he's marching. To learn, first march in a line. I eat one cookie. My hunger meets the cookie pain reflects back. Pain at the far side of hunger scoops out the stomach pit destination of chocolate marching schoolboy. The boy learns in a pit school. Here's his fenced yard. Here black asphalt they force him run. Here steps they surround attack him. These the footprints of evenly-marching boy, drops of blood brown-dried, vomit brown-dried. Acid. And black door silver sign *Cafetorium*. Smell memory of grease-burnt balls of chocolate-dark meat strong like still baking in slide projector heat.

Slam the white door, sick. Lights out. All lights out. Not hungry now. And don't care to learn any further.

How I grew up here, how I went to school here, took jobs here.

How I am still here.

Does it hurt? Walk, walk around, walk it out.

Streets same exactly last year. Candyland stopped ache stop. Itself-digesting Candyland.

Sprinkle Topping warehouse bricks candyapple gone to airbrown tomatojuice. Between bricks all mortar darked-out gaps spider-lines. Boarded windows rot open up black space within hollow, air pours out cold. More bats of brick in yard each year more broken boards, trash *result* thrown off by building denying building.

Magnificent industry *Fair-Lee Jawbreaker* bankrupt. Black low maze plant broken stucco show-through lath brown teeth. Dead buildings, because Fair-Lee adhered to life so stickingly, still trying to speak: **they come in nine colors but all taste the same**

Many worked here, slowly turning to soft powder. **add condensed milk 9 to 5 and extrude your future** say the ache buildings **it takes a food to make a food**

Ghost Fair-Lee ambition all that keeps cheap buildings upright. Jawbreakers that last longer longer longer, world's slowest to die, the Seven-Day jawbreaker: here was re-invented stone. **never bite down**

The taste of pebble. Unwary children and dour orators bought for years of languish till Fair-Lee's second idea: *big* size of handball jawbreaker. Biggest In World. Burned in sugar and dyed black by baffled workers.

Shards of jawbreaker shrapnel beside loading-dock cinder wall, workers loved to hurl the new Big model and it shatter. The Biggest In World would not fit into a human mouth.

Somebody forgot what candy was for.

I used to remember how to spend a day by myself.

Miss Nobel implies I have no fire in the belly. Why not get a regular job, I hate to see you living like this, she says it's down to my self-opinion. Says a person's got to eat.

Everybody has tried to eat.

Old gas station finally died. Somebody else made it a car lot six used cars for sale, became a place of six abandoned cars. They still sit. Little cube building across the road from there got a fresh seeming of brown-plastic brick, for a year attempted manufacture *Polar Explorer* the candy like a foil-wrap sphere mint-ball of snow, except not cold. These never made it to store because kept changing flavor in wrapper, mint by week three tasted of cough syrup, three weeks later snow-candystuff already brown, flavor broken down to sour of old blood.

Snow-white mint soap smear-covering glass door. Building ache corpse Explorer.

Jellybabies Motel that's alive. Out behind it

long sandcolor metal shed used to be Tesla Confections frizz-hair old guy technique electrodes into syrup to fry sugar to peppermint glass. Tried selling this broken glass clear candy wintergreen razor sharp edges till shut down by New Jersey officials. The shed tin roof rust blood, windows all dust glass back to sandstone.

Tar black flat elementary yard for play, behind it high barn of the deaf man. He molded maple sugar statues: a forest of little maple trees in square of maple earth, a steam-train in sweet rock, a city sugar skyscrapers. Each confection sculpted set to harden by the window. People did buy sometimes but who really could eat a whole sugar forest or six-pound maple train.

The deaf man stopped by death sculpting. Diabetic his legs digested, then his eyes. Deaf man who was scandal artist, bribing the kids through schoolyard fence. Paying big shards his leftover maple rubble waste to get them lined up in tight file, so hidden he could lie on the ground, squirm off his clothes, and naked stare up at the kids' mouths, mouths screaming unison reading always same words off his index card WORM-FUCK-WORM-FUCK! Writhe staring at mouths, trying to believe he hears the voices.

But I smell chocolate.

Three wings of abandoned building, but center blue cube still being used. The sign used to neon flash WINKS. Winks round blobs of chocolate flat like crushed kisses, called Winks because

Hershey owns the name of Kiss. When sued by British Winks Ltd, the neon sign came down replaced by this sad blue printed BLINKS.

Three abandoned wings of building because Blinks is not such a good name. Wings stand dark dead legs and dead skull. But torso building yet living life out, emitting the sweet burned air causes workers dub the place Stinks, and even I worked one summer here. Still smell it in me.

I was a Blinks Guide, final surviving factory tourist tour in Candyland. Up the one ramp down other, all tourists love wear cameras, snapshots evidence throughout America of me in my factory.

Sanitary stainless steel my mouth saying that, photo blink flash

Highest quality cocoa nib saying that, blink flash

I prop my arms around two generous-eating hat-shape-skull ladies dots for eyes, my face pale bounces back extra flashbulb

(I *blink* eyes shut in their pictures makes extra product awareness)

Tiny children take these small candies which allegorize inattention, bring blankly to mouth and suck, flash

Waving my arms frozen. Brown candy filth blurting out pipe into vat bowl. I'm talking, chocolate ambrosia angel miracle, candy liquid behind me blooping and spurting

Poor Dinah still works here. Not me. I meet her after work because the Cardinal's face hated me, I have to see friend face.

Photograph Dinah's hand flat spread fingers on coffee-shop table. Close-up fingers each with its own ring bandage, four flesh bandages where rings would go. Assume she burned herself at work, she runs Blinks chocolate-liquor vat, press three buttons and scrub clean the metal. Blinks is where I met her. Holding her fork, a picture bandages, and tines fork and fingers. I can't eat. Dinah's sauerkraut, black bread, a dish of pickles. Grapefruit juice. Our work lunch menu, only stuff you can force down during anti-food air in every breath of sick chocolate lung. Her bandaged fingers ripping open black bread, picture.

Finally ask trivia how'd you hurt your fingers?

Oh, hm. Yeah, cut them. On glass. Oh the mirror broke. I hit it, and it broke. Punched it. Shattered all over the place. Everything's OK, it's fine. I just sort of got frustrated, well it got his attention. Everything's fine now. He's learning...I guess. No, we're fine.

A picture I think and never take because never see: her boyfriend in their apartment, never seen their apartment, her boyfriend at their piano. Never do meet that boyfriend. He *not working* feeding upon her stole her saving money to buy this piano, twelve fourteen hours every day he attempts write terrible Broadway tunes show based on Webern tone-rows, lyrics life story of Pound, Ezra. Puts Dinah headache methane fog. She says he used to be a human.

Dinah in my trash discard kitchen home, then looking at my extra kitchen. Sitting in my extra kitchen. Very quiet here, no piano. Zero piano.

Dinah screaming singing in my other kitchen, on her stomach bellowing forced-memorize notes tunes piano Ezra twelvetone *Bahn-bahm bah-hah-hahum! BAHM, ba-BUP! Tinkle tinkle tinkle trummm.*

Says: she's upset/doesn't care. That just a *musical illustration.* Won't talk about. Is fine. Sitting in my other kitchen. Staying night, just to stay away.

Sitting in my extra kitchen on a new mattress, got her clothes her books. A roommate is a fragile egg. Tells me has diagram of her life plans on paper sheet...she won't show me. I who live among nothing have a roommate, I have my roommate.

In solitude shine the Cardinal slide at a mirror, I can't see it. See me myself back of projector, and the blind white eye red fifteenth-century cassock light reflected back on my face trying to eat cookies alone in dark hidden.

So she can help. We *re-photograph* the Cardinal. Shine blast Cardinal stone block face onto Dinah's white cotton t-shirt chest in the dim; tripod picture her face that likes me, and below hers his. Her breasts make his orange head smear out into horns.

She takes off her t-shirt, his face goes livid wavering, pulls on a different shirt light silk. *That makes him look beautiful* I complain. Won't photograph his face ethereal shimmery so shirt off, brown new shirt, *no, now he's human sad suffering. Do you have a shirt, like, pig-iron?*

Graze warm smells after midnight, Chef downstairs experimenting with, air says, brazilnuts leaching tomatoed veal. I'm sitting on my countertop, spin-the-bottle I whirl a butcher knife around freespinning the center, and Dinah puts out her hand, not looking directly at knife, fist stops it. "That—" she's not looking, "that gets me dizzy." Knife pointing at her. She shoves it off counter, hits wood floor and point sticks.

Dinah's face, in the dim of the microwave light.

Good friend Dinah's face, I can't see what it thinks. I could say things she hates me for saying and not notice I wouldn't *see*. Blank "but what about your girlfriend doctor? She wouldn't be happy would she." Dinah's face and turning robot carousel of the microwave.

I push a button in empty air if her face a

fresh education slide it could shine drop click from the endless circle tray.

Microwaving restaurant leftovers casserole paper bucket rumbles in circle under the lightbulb. The timer doesn't feel any different to itself just because it's about to click off. Micro oven squat cold to the touch.

"I'm not going to stay here long," she says.

Below the stabbed floor the restaurant oven's all afire. Wide as pizza oven and taller, you could roll into and slam the metal lid after you. "I'll leave you alone," I say.

Across my kitchen across dark zone, in Dinah's own private separate kitchen, a moth swings around the paper lantern. That paper lantern property of my roommate. Without right I suck its light to my eye. I steal popping moth sound hide into secret ears.

In pitch night coming back from Miss Nobel's, climbing up carefully the fire escape. Whisper above is Dinah climbing out down, in foodless air she smells warm like a new pie, we clamber past slightly poke each other for reassurance. Hunger sidewalks rubble, black burned candylooking nuggets maybe rats dead starvation.

Tire roll sound and we freeze there on fire escape. Eater people disgorging from gunmetal sedan. Girl of banker-man falls against him, laughing her voice across night "Starving!" falling into his soft overcoat her hand claws his arm, not falling, shouldn't be called falling. Our fancy restaurant's popular, worth to get fed a girl's placing tips of her brown little boots into funny rubbly mess. Banker left hand in his pocket, girl right hand in her pocket, matched fingertips matched nozzle cans of pepper spray cocked till safe inside.

Girl looks up sees *us*. Her face jerks away bland. People actually live above this restaurant. People live like this.

I creep up ladder look in. Dinah has said *My friend David's here. I'll be right back.* Still a shock a *guy* in Dinah's kitchen. Doesn't see me crawl in he's intent. He's standing on her stovetop, facing back wall moving one conducting arm Mahler forte when I slide approach silent through my kitchen, he's drawing on high wall above her stove with purple marker pen four more pen colors sticking out his mouth two and two fat whisker cartoons. When because the drawing's a black goat legs-out drowning purple maelstrom I go *Wow*, the David guy spins around his own goat hoofs tangle, he staring at me falls off the stove, long long way to floor the way he does it, arms gesture spells everywhere markers flying magic.

Would be the David she met two years past in Mexico, she travelling alone he there with the wish to die. He rolled hugging self into surf. *True story* she told me it.

Now the three of us. New material presents itself to me, David visual his eyes skitter while Dinah's consider units of air between us. David visual wrist thumping his nose for *oh yeah* hands shake always blur slightly except if he's drawing, twitch becomes a direction of line, tremble a thick vibration gesture. David who makes Dinah visual alter almost serene, they fit together both so young new with their new skins visual faces eyes how they don't know yet.

New material (David) lifts his arms no smile. Where light stops arms disappear in black. Torso and half a face mouth whole knowledge dust, plenitude of dust mouth. Throat noise makes idea of flexing fingers higher dark. Avidly me clicking up pictures this young man's ripping-apart idiom,

we're startled and stop in Dinah sudden walking out dark into other kitchen leaving us alone, she's banging my darkroom stuff around, David says Dinah? she from black back there shouts WHAT?!

WHAT puts David sitting in Mexican summer dirt late night Uxmal. I photo him sitting there in eyes surrounded walls of stone palace carved decoration abstract. Uxmal reasoned astronomy and pacifist design of rock. He all night in little German rent-car along ruins roadway trundles

toward gulf coast, the ruins harshen. Slowly they're
carved with not patterns, carved with faces, gods.
Alone in night driedout jungle a tiny stone house
thick walls one tiny crushing room where fat giant
phallus of stone sticks out the stone wall directly
over the stone slab rape bed. Night drive to limit
gulf water edge, dawn pictures: carved skulls in rows
by the thousands, men carving stone skulls all their
lives under this same hollow sunlight rings into
David's head syrup. And when he was David's age
his head eyes ringing death sunlight they grabbed
him in stone story carving they cut off his head.
And snakes sprung up out of the neck like blood,
snakes all speaking the word for *Word*.

At noon that day sunlight finally happened
behind his eyes.

Where Dinah found him was so-called
Nunnery. Where young women are chained up and
raped for a year before their chests are knifed open
hearts ripped out and thrown beating into the stone
lap of CHAC-MOOL.

Dinah gave him her tray of carrots. The
flower-seller is looking, alms kids standing away,
David bent over stone floor cracking with his
forehead the tray, eating mashing with his skull the
offering carrots. Speaking of virgins to the stone.

David and Dinah touch with their hands the
inner lap of the god. Dinah says: try to understand
their culture, there's a thing called justice, people
who are wronged may punish. The whole culture
felt wronged.

David says: we depend on people to be gentle about their gods.

CHAC-MOOL says: I was born with my lap this empty bowl. *YOU* must give me to fill it.

Drawings startle appear. Reach to wash sandwich dumpster lettuce for the colander on the wall and behind it wall white paint scratched-away with scary nail, old layer orange paint under makes flame rocket mandala shooting at shattering a white-paint leopard with cat face of: I knew this.

Chop on their little cuttingboard a red dumpster onion, fingertips realize backside of board damage. It's gouged-out burned-in woodcut of a fried egg bleak still-alive on a plate, egg shines with wood rubbed and crushed-in makes your stomach fear the baby dead within all eggs. And border of carved eater faces looking in at victim egg one huge cinder hand holds butcherknife.

Painted train derailment on the oven door. While I'm staring forgot I was hungry saying how amazing I think David's work is, Dinah not hearing me's saying David's technique's not really developed, his rendering needs a lot of work. We say the word "work" same instant.

Roommates tear me out of pattern. Like waiting for night food leftover restaurant bucket, why not eat cook whole banquet our own? Suddenly *making dinner*, Dinah with wish *pizza* invents a recipe, youth lacking historical memory never heard of dough equals yeast-plus-time, so she serves up a white flat cracker seared through by bright red eye of a tomatopaste helicopter spotlight, how would she know spices/olive oil? cracker Australia-shape pizza all-beamed on one primary-color flavor, acid harsh and clean. Break pieces of this off in mouths and chew we call it pizza, I photograph their faces eating talking. Sprawled on kitchen floor cracking shard pizza from the cookie-sheet washing it with tepid Pernod white plastic toothbrush cups, the licorice and heat at jawbone and behind the nipples blending with the pseud pizza how gray Necco wafers go with root beer, simply extreme: we say yum, we're hungry. Their faces clean intense no historical memory like now sitting eating together might be life.

Then ceremony unlid my pot of beans. Beans scooped out of the pot by three teaspoons communally: I take David's picture. David bites down. The picture rescues the last moment before his mouth has tasted the vastly complex black-bean stew-bile-surprise, extra-depth-knowledge several hours in cook, secret uniquifying ingredients orange peel and fenugreek. They look at each other. I take my own bitter, horrible beans bite as David tells me mm Jim, what an interesting serious taste *yes it is* as Dinah shouting him down laughs what? what are you *saying?* this is fucking horrible! Can't quite see Dinah to photograph now, she's humiliation visual filter fog yellow acid. A pause. I fail the pause. Cannot say words *gaak, throw these beans out the window!* no I take another bite, I'm not talking. Which David upset for me way too much takes *handful* of beans and eats them bent over, scary we don't laugh, me and Dinah look at each other. Because she can't be nice to my horrible beans, because she's right, because I want them to be called good but only if *believed* good (I could if undisturbed make a case for not throwing this pot down the latrine, alone I might settle for these, might *like* the bullying taste equivalent to self-bullying of eating leftovers alone in the dark) because her non-ability to cook anyway's not uptight pretentious, because feels as for an old zoo animal sorry for me how I can't dance this dance of the failed beans, and now my fault David's gone weird dangerous off rails under bad mood of her final judgment power, she backs off gives benediction smile: Jim—beans—*so* fucking *harsh!* Youth slang compliment.

My camera's been drinking faster than me, slides into Pernod-induced hydraulics, pictures I take slant steady now like a gyroscope. The Pernod says the beauty youths are trying to find a way to like me. Says settle for that. David smiles capable again, glugs Pernod directly into the beans and *stirs*, because we're *hungry*, hey now it's not so bad! Isn't that odd. The thing is to enjoy it.

Dinah and David midriffs on my kitchen
floor, baby fat hers peach-fed unaware, his grazing
peachfuzz. I have to be younger *beat them* at youth
atmosphere charm sheath. They could help. They
could pretend it makes me [my now lost decade
need for radio voice beside my ear to bear fall asleep
alone] a youth puppy in cardboard box whimpers
without mother heart of zeit, geist, clock, tick.

Opportunity sneak over and riffle through
their papers, her journal of tense visits to her farm
parents, of an irritating-to-her Harrisburg pie-eat
contest, her journal: in which I go *completely unmen-
tioned*. Each page I photograph with tiny silver
Minox spy camera, lacking trenchcoat I steal a
David baseball cap. In case they catch me on my
head my alibi: blame David I'm David.

Unroll a friendly privacy barrier between our
kitchens—hanging sheet of mylar silver to duck
under—keep us private except at night works like
one-way mirror—I can look right at them looking
right at, seems, me (combs her hair in it). Stare at
them. Story I don't know.

I brighten shine my lights to open the mylar
mirror from one-way to two. Sideways glancing
through it with spotlight on me, slow realize they
never watch me through the thing. Like I'm not
their business.

Mexico, story I don't know. I want to be
there too. I cut construction paper, make of chewed

gum a Chac-Mool, crayon snakes and skulls, sunrise-lightbulb tabletop photo close-up Mayan, thimble Tulum in an infinite platter of ink-grayed milk. Further ruins I just shoot pictures wandering out in courtyard.

Very late nighttime I sneak shine project these slides through the mylar into their kitchen. Mexico dim-papers the whole room, decal floor-sleeping visible portions Dinah and David with made-up terror-religion crux props. But have to see *me* sitting alone with slide machine mirrored back. I've never been to Mexico. Never been out of town.

Take stealthy the mylar away and hang a gauze white curtain, shine these slides. Mexico structures on the net curtain scrim. Beyond glow lit-up themselves snoring, extra trapped alone. Better.

On my kitchen floor, hold slide projector exhaling in my arms, chin against the blowing vent. Shine David's face straight into the face of a potato. Gouge I make on his terrible wounded cheek is only the eye.

Showing off old photos of mine, can't get them to admire me. Pretext of asking for democratic critique, old great art younger-Jim moment photos lying at Dinah's feet where she's tossed them.

I place in my mouth, under the eyes of Dinah and David, a tiny fortifying black chocolate baby.

"My pictures maybe aren't realistic," I say. "They're maybe not for everybody." Old photos of mine I was sure were really cool. "Not for anybody," she says.

The meeting midair of a white liquid and a black, above a sheet of spun steel, robotic/organic scary, she's printed crayon along the bottom: *Ugh. This is so angry.*

A picture of nothing but a wall, blank gray darkening at edges, and a whiff on all four edges of something cut-off, metal-thing you can't see, black thing you can't, wood edge thing, person edge body thing at right.

It's moving, if you're clued-in you're moved by inability. But on this void wall Dinah drew a yellow crayon rectangle, inside that rectangle drew vase and scribble flowers, hung her picture on my empty wall.

Because a photograph is supposed to be OF someTHING, she says. And you put the THING in the middle, so people can SEE it.

Sixty good prints she's marked up like that.

Dark dark glow stars floating over deep gray watersunk knife blades and spoons, this a close-up of downstairs rubble corner, shot in whole day but printed so night dark you have to hold your breath and stare in to reach it, Dinah wrote across this *Why not totally black while you're at it?*

Do I suck give up pretentious crap really suck? Oh David good understander artist please defend me. He's looking at a blackened tilted

Candyland vista: "They're hectoring," he says, "I wondered where's the Jim I knew. I thought you were a nice guy."

Oh but I have their faces. I have by dozens. Search through Dinah faces six hundred proofsheet pictures: waiting little face blanking bland. *One* picture, the slip accident, Dinah irritated contemptuous staring into dark. Her chin a chopper, cheek-blades white. Blow *this one* picture up huge, it is the *interesting* one.

Then David. David supposed to have "gone mad" in Mexico. Search for harsh picture of him too—but they're *all* harsh. Six hundred pictures of his face, it scares me confusion, hundreds *separate* expressions pain exult stress glitter-joke folded-within. *A barrage.* A barrier I can build. Riches.

Albion has us over for dinner.

He explains his bedroom:

Here is where his girlfriend sat. That's why it's so spooky a corner of sofa. That's why the air does what it does around this spot.

I photograph this. Dinah looks at it. David sits down in the sofa holy spot.

It's comfortable, he says. Dinah tugs at him but he won't get up. I'm feeding this piece of air, he says. Pulls her onto his lap, they laugh and roll.

I deserve that, Albion says.

Albion is trying to explain: "If I say I killed her I'm ridiculous. Because when I exaggerate and make dramatic story out of it, I feel her go flat. She becomes connect-the-dots, the more ARTICU-LATE I get, the more I say *So in rejecting her I cast her to her death.*

"Her dots want to converge and talk. Almost worse than if I *did* kill her, for me to sit here and force her dots together, make her say stuff like 'Don't feel bad, Al, it wasn't your fault, you terribly honest self-lacerator, why you've suffered worse than me!'

"Lie. She suffered death. All I did was we broke up, I was a jerk and she was not, I wouldn't even accept 'Do you want me to leave?' no I forced her to say 'I'm going to move out,' I made sure it was HER DOING.

"She left and she went somewhere. I didn't care where she was.

"Next month she was murdered. By an old boyfriend of hers. And then I want to say WHO I FORCED HER BACK TO. Because I want the focus on me. I resent her dramatic flame-out.

"I won't even talk about what happened.

"But I want you guys to help me have dinner. This experimental dinner. Sort of séance.

"I've been reading Wedekind and Büchner, trying to get a dinner voice for Gwenna's murder. I don't know quite what I'm doing yet. Make a dinner that's idiotic. Because I was an idiot. Trying to get a thick-tongued style to match one's grief."

David says "One's?"

Dinah "We brought some food potluck...will that mess up your *concept*? We're pretty starving."

Albion "No it's good, part of the event, for right now I accept everything. I'm just sometimes going to take a few notes, don't be annoyed by it. Ideas occur to me."

David mutter to Dinah, "Gwenna dead still loves him. And he says he's trying to *match grief to a style.*"

Big milk-glass round tabletop, we're sitting low on wicker stools around. I can make of it if I stand and shoot a close-up curve of water-drop with the waiting fingers of Dinah. Another scoop of glass moon with isolated David quivering hands. Or shoot into source light it's Albion neat stack notecards and his pudgy gestures more speech than curve of glass is mute, even.

I unbag what I brought, vodka with hot-pepper juice I've soaked and squoze in, this looks like vodka but's napalm clear and calm, in fun I don't warn anybody careful. I'm taking their pictures getting set to drink the evil stuff out of little shotglasses, Albion for art-ness directs me to crayon draw on the milk-glass tabletop a "photograph" that goes with my food, I can't draw so I draw with black crayon two black curve pointed shapes and empty cube between. Cube about to be pierced.

David about to sip says, it's violence, and I continue to not warn him about pepper vodka. Instead of speaking warning, I *see* him. I take his picture and he gulps it, again I take his picture. Pain of the pepper down his throat roaring back into his whole face through roof of mouth, this pain comes high speed from far away, and I take the picture. Pain dropping down on him, he knows it's the change he always fears (that solid floor is unreal, what keeps him here not here) I'm taking take take take. My camera sees sweat, far-eye fuzz, fingertips wavering hopelessly for the surface of table. Knowing how he feels makes me turn camera vertical to make space above him arrival space of falling terror. Fear comes from outside because it's real, but comes right *to* David because it's David. Speed of zooming-in fear makes him photogenic. Albion's taking notes like crazy.

Dinah's blocked-off David, she's in the way of camera.

"Are you OK?" I say smile.

He was staring down through tabletop and now that I can't get clear shot of him I look too: our legs down there through the white glass, dark impurities in the milk.

David and Dinah hidden back in corner, out of range. I'm concentrating on the dish of art-food been placed before me, sog brown-bug swamp of mulberry leaves steamed, sprinkled with dry unmistakable marijuana (also derives from mulberry family, concept us supposed to eat and then like worms commence be able spin art silk). I love the plate of impossible grub and shred it into mouth wishing for stinging nettles, iron filings. Albion has discovered negative food! Want to congratulate him but he's *speaking*:

Albion GWENNA: I'm sorry...what's happened to you? You're scaring me! Please say something!

[lines from his roughdraft Performance Dinner, intends eventually force eaters to play these parts]

Albion ALBION: (singsong) I can't just say Yesssss you blonde body, every Yes has a No! I need a miracle from you: walk out on me! Rise above!

[roles for his dead Gwenna and for the murderer of her, and for Albion himself]

Albion GWENNA: *I don't know who I am anymore.*

Albion ALBION: That's a fine start!

[Albion as his own past self from last year he this year sees and attacks as *new better judge art self*]

Dinah returned to table rock serious sitting in her spot. David down low drawing on glass tabletop very small in felt wet red pen, licking his hand like cat and wet-destroying as he draws, hand all blood ink.

I don't dare take a picture with Dinah looking at me. I see six pictures pass lost untaken, *terrible*. Results me staring at wall shadow of myself seeking image, photo I take of shadow of me:

Blurry huge stone bird top of man-carved cliff. Light stone wing blotted out in bulk heavy teetering smash bird crushing blackness. Print that dark darker. Tilt the frame print worse yet.

Dinah not in the mood to play will not serve up her potluck contribution. So Albion ladles it out: chopped potato chunks, each tumorous different, mine like a baby jogging shoe brown with ankle attached and drawer-knob on ankle. She won't eat her own food, even.

Dinah does hand over an index card on which she's written, by order of dinner host director, her statement.

When I play basketball I am not drinking.
When I ride my bicycle I am not telling lies.
When I plant vegetables nobody can betray my
trust.

These globs of cornmeal food meant as hushpuppies, but she fried in black coffee. I'm making nice little banter jokes about it, banter banter light so friendly and nice I permit myself all smooth in fun to take pictures of David again. David's face twisted glassdown to keep anchored. Blinking drawing licking erasing. Each time he blinks I click.

Albion puts hand on David's red hand, so unerased drawing stays. It's cartoon of Dinah serene at the center of lines tornado vortex. Dinah laughs. Why don't you draw me, I say. Albion writes something down. Well he never draws me, I say.

Dinah is *fine*. Glazes when photographed she

ignores me, but that's better than furious, yes she's fine again we're fine. David all over the room playing with the centrifuge canister or laying his head on the little anvil, really likes being photographed I think, I'm on my fourth roll. Albion orders David's *statement* be delivered in words so David crayon draws words on perimeter of the stewpot

> *need some meat*
> *in weightless space?*
> *the birds you eat*
> *are flightless*

This David's potluck, mélange of broiled bird-meat in stew, *real food* stew deep in five colors and sticking out dimestore toothpick flags-of-all-nations. So instead of puke play joke, we all dish piles of adhering juicy vegetables cheese and birds, it binds with strings of white, visual *yum* I photograph my food.

I photograph my food and my own hand on fork.

Can't eat.

Dinah's face is a girl's beautiful face. She loves David with his crown of dark lamp edge shadow, his laugh of mouth despair. Albion demands a statement from me, I say *Goethe:*

When confronted with great superiority in another, a fellow's only recourse is hatred.

Dinah looks like to say that's not how the quote

goes, but doesn't bother. She doesn't care, didn't choose me. She chose this person who's unstable brilliant shining more silver.

Albion MURDERER: You empty piece of youth. You pre-killed little beast. You can't leave me again, you hate your Albion, I love your flesh, I want your hair you are a *horror*. You can't love don't know how—you love me, you love parmesan cheese—you need me, you need a new pair of shoes. You never love me *with myself*—you don't have my strength. You're so beautiful! I want to love myself and you're not helping *weakling*. If I ate your body I'd feel pretty, such a dish.

Albion GWENNA: I—

Albion MURDERER: *SHUT UP STOP IT*—I CAN'T STAND THE STUPID NOISE—I NEED PEACE OF MIND—OK—OK. OK. Are you going to shut up? Don't speak. OK. Fucking you is not enough owning. That's your builtin fault. You can't give me enough so I'm going to have to die. I can't stand it: *I'm* going to have to die and it's *your fault*.

David's saying Wait, I don't get it. She was really your girlfriend. She really died. Why are you writing a play?

Albion explains his play's about beauty in the world, beauty commodity, beautification manipulation, what beauty's consumed for, what it does to people. David saying *mm*. Drawing and rubbing-out on the edge tabletop *rim*. David an eye that rim razor milk edge slices its face in photograph.

Albion says: what question are you really asking me?

David at table slipping confrontation, immune to me clicking him, eyebrows evading Albion, watching Mexico. He draws big on table picture of me, that's *my face* he's taken! he draws each line of my face with his own flesh hand, no machine but the pen stick, took my face in through his eyes out his fingers. And my face he gives a body of wood cubes, my own body wood or maybe block rocks lying in a bed. Lying beside this ME is Dinah sex curvy but joke hair, lying on other side is David himself with same vague curvy girl body. And a slashmark speaks out of my mouth says *What do they think of me?*

David walking out into the water at Tulum, cliff behind him, top of cliff stone teeth of temple terrifies boat tribes. A wall that looks lethal like fortress yet is holy temple. This picture shot from farther out in the water, aboard a pleasure craft. David water to waist just wading. Next picture a head treading water. Next picture, David gone from the world.

Wait for click. His face is fine, pleased talking, he's acting up for Albion's eye,
    now click David his mouth gaping. Eyes shut. This was part of a laugh but. Cheek flung at ceiling light, twist neck hair skew. Because I care about him, because *concerned.* His arm white a blob snake.

Because scary things are always true truth always good.

He's black on the easel, light is black milk. Shadow room dark around him in negative all white lights up my darkroom.

He's little black chip flat, all of him under my fingertips. And I am made of cubes.

Albion: What are you really asking me? Say what you mean. Hey we're all friends here!

Albion: Then I direct you to ask questions.
Jim: People who ask questions don't know.

Albion: Do we necessarily all agree that purity is a higher value than impurity?
Dinah: What would prevent a guy from knowing he's corrupt?
Jim: Why is a hungry man, if bit by a hungry serpent, more likely to die than if they both had breakfast?
David: Do you love me? (Dinah: Yeah.)
Jim: Any of you love me and if so why?
David: I remember I was completely happy pushing higher and higher a pile of sand at age six so is that any protection? (Dinah: No.)
Albion: Was the resulting sandpile permanent and excellent?
Jim: Is the light hitting sand the actual ideal sand? What'll I do with ideal sand "distill" it, is that *clearer*? Like water's a truer food?

David: Should my headache worsen if pain is truth? Am I coward to keep evading being not alive? If you finally punch through my throat with a spike will my grin look less fake sickening to me in Hell?

Jim: This insoluble conflict: shall I do without, or go ahead steal the roast pig and gobble?

Dinah: Sounds like you want to steal the pig: where's the conflict?

Jim: It's so much *more complicated* than that simple moralism, it's the *anguish* of not knowing how to *act*.

Albion: Is that a question or an answer?

Dinah: Are you in "pain" black liar?

Jim: My stomach hurts. I mean Don't you believe my stomach hurts?

David: Your faces have futures.

Nobody speaks. He makes it a form of question.

I'm whole time photographing constantly drawing light off him. But I never direct him, never force or falsify. That's what I tell myself I appreciate about me.

I'm way in room back farthest corner from table, Dinah's head blocking carefully like Japanese fan my view of David face, and light only shines in light zone areas, *conditions are hard*. I click (a click a tiny thing) click only when I can glimpse a click of theory, click David saying It's dark, now. I'm blind almost.

click Dinah pleading him please just don't let Jim see any more of your drawings.

Depth in the room, all the way out to the vanishing point, David sucks that to him and draws these flat lines. You can't anymore walk into it once he's done. (click)

David saying People see the drawing so I erase it. I can't do it to them.

Quietest clicks. He speaking not speaking "I drew carvings and pyramids in Mexico—rendered like a camera machine—until—it became absolute I had to walk into the sucking distance I made. *Scribbled over my pictures* I was safe back on the paper again. Relief—till—I looked at the weeks of drawing work — — — scribbled lines."

Not speaking anger "Jim wants me to swallow food for him. Every night he's alone says What's out there I'm so blind somebody tell me answers. But with us friends competes who can ask questions unanswerable. The way I draw is the way he photos, he claims claiming me—oh wild and transgressive.

"But I will live if I can have perspective get clear lucid. Be alive if I can make hard edges be the picture, so everybody can look say What control. Jim praised me the way my work kept *falling apart into abstract, almost self-swallowed* and I smiled held my throat open, *don't gasp*, panic jumped and I smiled blink blink, the room dims when you blink it back, people flatten, what they say to you goes onto skin tattoo, it sticks hardens on the flat world. Stuck with it. Noplace to throw it *in*."

(Taking his picture. Well he permits it. I think he enjoys. How do I know he hates it if he never tells me?)

"You keep looking. *Huddled-by-the-table* I'm *pain-in-eyes*. Stripped gears, oh right you don't *see* that. Pictures so you can trap my scum-open face. Show how I stare at your camera thinking *Please don't*. If only I'd kill myself add to your picture value authenticity. Brave photog who crawled among suicides. Meanwhile store up the sucking spaces around my head. Express yourself Jim. You know I can't tell you to stop. I don't want a photo of me telling you to stop."

David *naked on floor nobody else in room Head turned to one side   Head turned to other side Turned over on stomach. Tight curled-up   Fingers grabbing for anything to cover himself, no   Camera floats right above   It, machine, takes every picture.*

David writes captions for my last roll of pictures:

1. Whore-boy whore-boy whore-boy whore-boy
2. Whore-boy whore-boy whore-boy whore-boy #2
3. Cocaine cocaine cocaine cocaine cocaine
4. Question question question question question
5. Runaway RUST.
6. Rubadub RUNT.
7. Slut-dick. Coke-slut-dick-boy.
8. Burn. Swill. Burn. Wallow. Burn.

9. Septum. Liver. Fire. Cigarette.

10. Cigarette-burn, cigarette-burn for eyes, eyes wet on me.

11. Faggot-whore, NURSE! Asshole-slave, ANSWERS!

12. Birds twittwittwittwittwittwittwittwittwittwit-twittwittwittweeeeeeeeeee.

13. Eeeeeeeeeeeeeeeeeeeeeeeeeeeeeeeeeeeeeeeeeeeeeeee.

14. Hollow pus-drum question eat answer not yours.

15. Mopsy hair pie boy chew up what they see of you.

16. Snow light freeze ingest ice condemned meal.

17. Know where they know you stand they change their tune twittwittwitt

18. Scribbly lines to sound pitch down

19. Scrape scrape make my me mine

20. Liar-cigarette-burn liar paper arm paper leg

21. Dead-language inner voice daub face puppet

22. Stripe stigma notches branded

23. Lens fish sun

24. Death blind gone-planet color-dead-color

Thank you! Keep the wound green! Make sure photo me! Frame a dark box! And the shadow? And smirch? Blear? Wall-eye squint? Dissolve eclipse?

Relax? OK? Nothing to worry about? Calm down? Come here? Come with me? Shh? Shh?

Dinah covering David's eyes with her hand and helping him stand up, Dinah murmuring to him, her other hand she put on his stomach, deliberately I kept taking pictures, voice she couldn't scream at me to stop else make things even worse, helped him out the door click my camera clicking away on purpose.

Then nothing.

I see what you're doing, says Albion, interesting, taking David apart, you have a fast eye, vicious, when I hear the click I've just started to see what you already saw coming, terrifying.

Night has come, out the window is the other world, flat black no deeper than windowglass.

With light I could destroy the film. Since I would not bullybastard stop, now I could at least apply can-opener to spools film and unwind them across the glass table, destroy the film with light.

That could work, says Albion—he writes it down notecard—that could be your final gesture, expose all the film like cutting your hair off, ashes on your head, like remaining silent, drowning your camera. That'd be beautiful performance expression, I'll use it. God poor David. I hope he's OK. Wasn't he amazing?

No, says Albion. *Christ* he says, you mean you're actually going to *do* that to your film?

Well I understand, says Albion. Listen, wait.

I just feel that it's a gesture, says Albion. You could do it, and it wouldn't matter to anybody but

you. That's meaningless. That's *self-indulgent*. You're
not here to destroy pictures are you? Like a doctor
who kills? Are you a doctor who executes people by
injection, just because you think they're "evil"? The
pictures are alive—let fate destroy them, or not.
You *keep on working no matter what*. If you're upset
make use of it.

Don't take this stuff so serious, you want to
be like David? I mean you think *he's* gonna last?

Downstairs a fat man, no one to help him eat.
Entire spread of new potatoes aged beef mint
jelly, salad and squash, a wine almost black ruby, fat
man's eaten every single thing. Waiter removes
plates, all but the tall slim glass of water. To the
water waiter adds a cowskin-wrapped bill.

Tablecloth spotted stained with crumbs of
vegetable and glob fat. Fat man stuffed alone suddenly starts scraping fat judo hand-edge all crumbs
off table, *flicks flicks* fingernail at the sticky bits,
scours gray stain with his vowing fingers. Then
wipes hands with the napkin on his tent lap, throws
napkin right on floor. Stares at water glass and the
bill. Waiter comes, for free refills his glass.

HARM, I mean FIRST, DO NO HARM.

(Miss Nobel reminds me the creed.)

Mercy Hospital corridor into Mercy Hospital room. Dying woman. It would be better if I didn't have eyes.

(We were talking about life support.)

Dying woman's lips move. My lips flutter, I'm making an *answer* to a person about to die. I'm saying she's beautiful, I'm saying her granddaughter loves her, she's going to forget I said that. She watches my mouth, I'm in her last nightmare. But she won't remember, she'll be dead. *I'll* remember. That's why I don't say "Just scoot your butt over."

(I don't want to see this either.)

Do Not Resuscitate. Because she was going to undergo undue financial hardship staying alive. It wasn't worth the amount of money.

(But I wouldn't want to live as a suction tube monster, I'd rather you pull the plug.)

Lying in bed as a potato doesn't make the economy money's worth, it doesn't make the wheels grease. And we aren't monuments worth preserving. Because we don't do enough. Our lips kiss. Red wine, we shoot owls, purchase flags and other goods, and we wait.

(But our lips kiss.)

We take a bath, I learn what your hair does wet, what your feet do, I never saw that before. But that's all I do, learn. You, you photo every kiss with your mind, so you're getting some value from your two eyes. Maybe you're worth preserving. I have too many eyes. People die every day of nothing. Specks, little cells, soft things. Kill. Routinely.

(You had a hard day.)

A car crash is a hard day. What if they lowered the speed limit to 20? Nobody would get body destroyed ever again crashing.

Except we all agree the horrible boredom driving slow's *not worth it*. Boredom. Like living in a hospital for years, and you're only 12. Kid where his intestine has to be removed a foot each operation, shorter and shorter. Finally can't digest anything for the rest of his life. We feed him on a drip. He gets infection in one vein we move to another. Finally he runs out of good veins. Operation, drip connected directly to his heart. He will get infected there. His final infection, his heart. Heart stop beating.

Then we *fight* to revive him.

He produces what value he's only 12. He naturally'd've starved and died years ago without all the money-costing operations and IV torture. Was he bored? Didn't seem bored. On-edge. He made remarks, bleak, sort of float in the air a second like awful and then you realize it's hilarious.

(Do Not Resuscitate.)

Too hard on a family to get them to sign DNR. They feel like murderers. Mercy Hospital has *abolished* DNR.

(I want to die in a worldwide apocalypse.)

Instead we have a new *name* for it. SUP-PORTIVE CARE PROTOCOL. Doesn't that sound pretty-much OK. Request Supportive Care Protocol

II...that is death. It doesn't *say* death on the piece of paper. It says pleasantly we promise to make the patient comfortable.

(Did a lot of people die today?)

Are you comfortable? How's your picture art mental sensibility? How's your stomach? Are you hungry?

(...)

Ambrosia. I would feed you ambrosia if that was what you wanted.

What died in my courtyard? I squeeze through ripped link fence stop scared. Shadow inside latrine too black. Little black spots on the car hood, sun jumps off metal and my stomach dips. Black spots in my eyes symptom 12.

Little black spots everyplace. Blink they live and blink persist.

Spots are real spots. Each a tiny black drawing. Dozens of drawings along wall of building, more trailing up fire ladder wall, poxing around my window.

Thick lines heavy black tux and wedding hat on wisp-drawn white David his lower lip stuck out huge

Señorita dwarf with long pistol, mustache,

sitting naked on garnish platter

Bald man jaw deformed jut grinning swinging on a swing above slain leopards

Pregnant women, twenty aligned like tulips, heads being lopped off with edge of huge black book ADDRESSES

Pregnant dog lying in mud barking into the hole of an old guitar

Naked rolls of fat glutton his mouth hanging open throwing javelin through the body of a speckled bird

Lady wearing laurel wreath distorts elongated her lips horribly to apply black lipstick, her dual mouth half-blacked

Huge featureless black rock rises out of earth beside little toothpick statue of a windmill

Face shorthair woman puffs around eyes, flat cheeks, eyes stare noplace

Face beard old man looking upward disappearing squeezed mouth

Barn full of floating faces glaring angry at a dog, dog glares angry at the ground

Laughing dog gobbling mud, whole mud mountain ready

Man posing for the artist, confident proud sculpture-clothes suit fashion mag illustration except his trouser cuffs ripped open swollen bare flesh club bulbs for feet

Inflated women on cables huge like Macy's parade, some hold trombones

Pig smoking cigarette holding two compact discs up as breasts

The descent of hungry crows upon a pile of dead crows

Elegant standing man with thorn branches growing out of his face

Young pretty cop boy with a ponytail and badge carrying medieval iron shackles

Ten alleycats sitting listening to a lecturer turnip wearing eyeglasses

David lying in bathtub with tubes entering top of his head, and huge pig behind him, pig nostrils blowing into the tubes

Dim of my inside kitchen. Slow window light looks historic. Sepia air light that wants to be daguerreotype.

That's the light only. Things the light bounces off are already photos horrible. Full-of-themselves photos stick cluttery everyplace, "my" photos by "me" all dark as possible, like a wall's something to wall off, like light's only what helps people catch you. The pictures can't be seen because the pictures won't be looked at.

Sweat. Path from stomach into skull nerves sweating scalp. Sweat face path panic fear of death stomach-cancer-liver-cancer gnaw oblique wish to live: sweat body anger, slamming stuff around, hurry-up mix up a bucket of hypo, disgust at plastic cheap tools, path from want feel better to want still able to make pictures is obtuse want to live. Mine negatives for medication. Wish to still *want* to make pictures, wish to want to live.

David eyes closed face white flat. I take the beauty like pill. Caption I write across top of print in hypo from my rust-steel fountain pen, so it'll develop out white handwriting:

"Don't hurt me." He won't say it loud enough.

I pick strongest negatives. Forget myself I become swooping across proofsheets ether. My stomach far below in time where I'm not. I select the negatives that hurt.

The ones that hurt. They don't hurt me, I'm

ether, they rasp *the viewer*. I have a floating head
hugged to my cheek; he's *the viewer* he looks alongside me. When David Dinah fail to live, when they
shine face light exposed false manner, exposed
torture concealment manner, *viewer* sucks in his
breath while I'm laughing.

The ones that hurt I print them dark.
Scribble captions on each in the yellow light:

> Lookit him he knows his place
> She keeps him still by bending
> Feed me! Don't look!
> The houseguest's always hungry
> These were children once
> All smiles: the sportswoman
> Wife, come quick! The room is empty again!
> My foot deserves to die
> He caters to his ripe analyst
> Pain adores discomfort
> Afraid of Nothing

Putting the pictures in different shuffle.
Calm now, the faces of my two friends playing-card-
royalty (but they're my subjects) the smell of developer behind my eyes now the center of calm. Developer stains brown scythes under my fingernails.
Dinah and David a story I told. Even dig out old
close-ups I took of broken granite, I print two
granite slabs dark and write across

Press against your past
and

Here is my throat

Stones at beginning and end make *book* of photos, stones cool the characters fictional. I can talk to Dinah's real face and know why so frozen still: that's how I painted it. A painting you don't worry about her secret opinion of you. She thinks what you paint her thinking.

But her thumbnail while I talk is ploughing straight line down floorboard seam waiting. She waits. All my questions are answers *of course I don't know, I wasn't there, but—you must have seen the trouble he was in—why the hell drag him through more scary ruins, and he didn't know the language, and drinking night and day, you could almost predict he'd—*

To photograph Dinah's thumbnail, during my calm speech, to save my calm, does not save my calm. Her thumbnail digging at floor, her face stone saying David's fine now, doing very well, is OK, we're careful, fine, OK. A photo of her thumbnail. Because I see you thinking anti-Jim thoughts. Blow-up print *your neurotic thumb.* So if you won't love me I can blackmail. Love me now?

I tape up display this new batch of prints: David and Dinah with captions by me. New photos all over my kitchen bury previous layers of photo. Both my *subjects* have to walk through all the time to get in and out my window, pictures taped right around the *windowframe.* So, nothing   no reaction

Molecules of chocolate seep through stomach wall bloop into bloodstream make your blood cells stick together clumps. Blood all through your body goes sludge. Tiniest arteries in brain are completely stuck chocolate stopped, makes you stupid but jumped-up by rush of speed sugar. You're galvanized dimwitted heedless blowing brain cells ready to attack. I pop six more Kisses. Walk around my floor waltzing my stomach, swinging it on end of the foodpipe, tenderness, stomach tenderness blanks my head from hurting; it's my partner, stomach, where my heart is. I'm not thinking. Put the prints in big dark pile and waltz them over to Dinah's side of the dual kitchen, the easiest distance.

Dinah looks at me looking up at David's new drawing. And this is how a drawing works:

Whole ceiling black-paint slashmarks render three objects. One thick huge against two small, the two small are small round fat Albion on the floor praying to the small cube oven, his chin resting on open slab-door, face mouth open *howling*. The huge thing is Dinah. Dinah over against the long edge of wall, compressed crushed, her face horrible empty, clear of content, vague nose no mouth, the eyes just thick holes, hair rendered detail perfectly, her arms like paired tapeworms drawn each paint mark thick but broken in the middle. All she has on her big slash blank mouthless jaw is a goatee.

Dinah looks me looking drawing. When did we freeze as friends? So now I can't say, do you wonder if he anymore loves you? Can't say, I would find this, like, too humiliating. Can't I say? Why not just say. But I look at her and oh, our friendship *way* kicks in again, friendship agreement to skip over actual speech unfortunately (*Excellent* is all I say), when one of us is upset we permit other to *see* us, see back the calm one calm, *Excellent* I won't laugh at you, I wish you had a better life, I'm here.

Really I'm a good friend. I *am*. And so here is a gift. Distract you from troubles. *Here* I say.

"What's this?"

And I might just've said *buncha pictures*. Or *just for you private*. She'd've been able to pretend all snapshot nothing, but she asked a question and me so full of answers, what's this? This a *photo novel* title *Dwarf*, probably you've seen some of these pictures on my walls, this my good friend Dinah is a Work

where I *take* David's breakdown in Mexico that you practically caused by mishandling everything, I *take*

his crackup you never confessed me enough about and I *explain* like poetic rendering homage, like. Not really

Not *really* about you, you're just the actors in it.
Really not

about anything, it's

just

some pictures of you two. Which I might try to get
published I think-they're-pretty-good

Night

has

fallen so Dinah cannot look at dead photos in her
lap. Top photo close-up stone with words scrawled
"Press against your past" she seems to not see.

Says in her exact voice, no sign of night her
unchanged voice Well actually I can't look at these
right now Jim I'm just heading out to play some
basketball.

"MAYBE DAVID SHOULDN'T LOOK
AT THESE, IT MIGHT BE A LITTLE UPSET-
TING FOR HIM" first moment that's occurred to
me! so

Suppose she shows pictures to him.

And he looks, each picture. Each so careful made maximum bleak.

so "I'LL LEAVE IT UP TO YOU DINAH WHETHER TO SHOW THEM TO HIM, IT'S YOUR DECISION."

David reading each hateful caption.

Your decision Dinah cause that lets me off my own hook immediately plus maybe could get you *intrigued:* here's something for *us* that *he* can't handle.

(You know why I do this? For the sake of the thing. The photograph *thing, image* is very beautiful, I'm pleased and proud. It's *good work.* Analyze word *good.*)

Hi David: everybody is calmer than you. Everybody can plan their attacks. Everybody can kill you, nobody is afraid of you.

Hi David: we can say what we want right at your face. They can call you whatever. We can spread hate slime stories on you. This hate name-calling could probably be true.

No such thing as a friend you trust. Trust not real the way knife or gun is. You *know* you can get hurt. You *don't know* your fine pals will protect you.

Truth more important than you are. Truth about you is what we all decide.

Not burdened-looking, Dinah puts pictures in a big grocerybag, moving around me in curved paths collects her bike helmet, sneakers, moves back to the wrinkly brown bag, flattens by smashing and stuffs it up on way high shelf, but talking normal. Only weird thing she says is I'll talk to you soon Jim.

Well of course you will. We're kitchen friends. You're stuck with me.

Basketball. A game.

Basketball, a ball.

Dinah rising. Her torso on its way up bangs into two skinny other girl players' faces. When stops rising she'll flip ball off her fingertips. On her way up she's a tense object which she must force through resistance *hard smooth*.

A game played in the dark, one lightbulb. They see half their struggle half black shadow. They leap into black zones.

Fingertips at the silent middle. Delicate in the noise. The object (ball) floats away from the object (Dinah).

Now another woman's jump grabbed and passed the ball both hands over her head. On her way down, this player catches Dinah's forehead with elbow, knocks her down on the night asphalt. Dinah sprawling out is already in scramble of standing back up, she's concentrating on not stopping. Suppose David die.

He's not strong. He is living with, in the kitchen adjoining, his tormentor. Tormentor exposes him like this: he broadcasts: wig-out nut I know, buy some pictures of him! Look what spazz drooling zombie. Look horrible *huge* wobbling face stuck on front of his brain. No lie no lie, camera doesn't lie.

So now you're a thing, good. Hi David now you're among us. People in the world all act like knowing things unto themselves. The chainlink fence doesn't look at you and say, I love you, I'm going to melt to let you through. It is a fence.

You have this very fuzz safety zone, who's holding the little netting? Your girlfriend, who's merely a woman you met once, and your two or three main friends.

Where are they then.

They are things.

Silent means they see you.

You can't be invisible clear. Cameras snap. You say Dinah save me Dinah. That saying is another *way* you have. "Dinah."

" "

Did you make her up? What do you know about her?

You know the springs not to touch cause they'll snap back and slice. Terror gray where you speak into it and nothing comes back out. Flat look with her nod she says

Why?

she says

Who cares?

Dinah   hates   you   David   she's one of the thing others. *Didn't you figure that out?* You are not even chainlink fence, you're a rag on the ground. You're these pictures of a white larva ridged worm. Everybody knows. They haven't stepped on you yet because it's too much bother.

Because you're still acting nice. You permit them bug document you.

If you stop acting nice.

If you're yourself.

If you roar now, who'll hear and come inject you with radium waste make your ugly whine shine for the world? Jim. Your girlfriend's friend Jim.

You try to talk *Thank you Jim a whole bunch for showing me my true self pal*, try act tough like they all can. Camera not fooled. Picture of you glaring right at camera, angry dust-eating zombie. Friend Jim scribble across it

IT'S HARD TO SEE   WHY

When did you look at him hating him? How did you know?

Or

How did he make you hate him visual? Why's he want to portray *flaunt* his shittiness betrayal?

Or

here's proof you are floating-hate-crazy bug fuzz

it's hard to see
why
wood floor is made wooden
wall to wall crack is straight line down
little spots you made on your cave
exposed in air can't hollow invisible
suck air down your throat
column of syrup down a pipe
slurp   gurgle

They drink you up. They suck you alive. All they had to do was see you: pegged you: liquid.

You drain out. Kill him for extra floppiness. Dead makes liquidy ease. Purée.

There will never be anything. Your eyes look at pencil: your hand will never be able to get out to pencil. You could not pull through the air towards you a pencil. That used to be easy because you were an idiot. No now way. Because pencil is color light, air cardboard air.

Now you're very still. Now we *take* your picture.

Now die stay still for us. Don't move don't blur. Stop. Freeze.

Still...life

Silent because

Forever because

Witness to the SHH witness to SHUT witness NO NO

SHUT UP! SHUT UP! SHUSH! HUSH! SHH!

whole gag body SHUT YR FACE

WE LIKE SOFT GENTLE PEACE DON'T YOU DAVID

EVERYBODY LIKES THE SILENT

You can stink, OK. Stink how you rot, how you like.

Have salt glop in back of throat if that helps you gag die.

Stifle suffoCATE! Can IT! Rubber gasket glass walls and lights. Photo terrarium for David frog-fungus-eyes.

Stop up that little noise that brain sound
that eeeee stop it you are jarring we want you potted

just rest just rest now, don't tax brain you
have a mental illness and must rest [STOP] the
affected part [DIE]

After you kill, you hear silence. Silence your
achievement, killing.

Sent pictures to attack objects. Achieved
blank no-image space.

Quiet in here.

Nobody home but me. David gone and
Dinah.

Their kitchen doesn't move. The air solid as
bread. My own kitchen looks at me, waiting. Squat
glum clubfoot oven squints. Inside of oven becomes
very still.

I kick oven and it withdraws from me.

Inside my freezer empty of all but ice. But
white air fog spins out into my open mouth. Freezer
moves, it breathes out.

On inside door of freezer I tape old painting
print: gilded lurid medieval Hell Mouth. The Hell
Mouth contains a whole party of eaters. Naked bath
couples in tubs together, wet twined feasting from
tub-tables. Cows with sex women's breasts lying
nearby forcing out with their own hoofs arcing

squirts of milk. On altar in mouth back, The Pope squatted buttocks his robes raised, he's laying green eggs in a golden bowl.

This living meal going on inside a huge open mouth with six-foot sharp teeth.

Mouth getting ready to bite all shut death silence. As it does. As it always does.

The mouth's got eyes up high in darkness. Eyes huge. Eyes stupid, with too much eating.

My freezer continues roll its breath out, never breathing in. It says: Ice dies, crack-crack.

David and Dinah silent because gone away. Silent because alive elsewhere.

Vegetables before sprouted look like absence. David lying still in wooden lawn-chair can look at his fingers and think of roots, he can dare his eyes two blackberries, but not dare look up at Dinah too much. She moves slow grim free across the empty lot. She's not connected up!

David's fingers, because attached to his mind, not permitted to sketch. They forge a chain net dead old wisteria vines, breaks if stressed.

I ate carrots Dinah grew herself, scrawny results from her ploughed squat of patch taken-over vacant lot. I know she told me cleared away busted glass trash rust, put up ownership bedsheets over old link fence. Then private world hoed out a circlet and made yellowish carrots. Hers, and she shared them among us. Now what I don't know: she's silent. Hoeing out the entire property. Sleeps there with David on the lawn-chair. She maintains him, he maintains, she maintains. She doesn't know what to plant or how quite to grow anything except carrots but seeds are cheap or free, she'll try plant everything, grapes, trees of fig, barrels of olives, cucumbers for pickle, potatoes every color. I don't know. I can't see it.

She plants seeds and David looks. The field is empty.

When weeds appear, she attacks and kills the weeds.

She gives water to the seeds *allows* them to grow.

There's nothing to see.

Eating   would be   blatant
Suck breath slow   through all teeth   do not jar the air
Don't look I'll do less damage
Shouldn't move. Shouldn't do things
Stomach gnarl confused, am I starving or sick
Unless I eat I die. That would be
No eat fat grease food corruption increase corruption

Crying would help leak grease but

Eat eggshells, pure

Eat ice cube   too pure to add rot to rot

I'm sorry. Required to eat. My fault

One slice white bread then.

One bite: sick shifts within me, bile leaps wanting to stain white of bread.

I see a fat Chinese grease duck dripping

Slice of white bread one bite gone. I sprinkle cinnamon on slice thinking I'm hiding it.

One bite I turned it into a TREAT!

I do not deserve this meal. So start adding more dust rain spices:

mint nutmeg mace   bite still too OK taste

ginger anise sandalwood   (pushing brown green powders in down)

scatter drops of almond milk

mustardseeds cloves a dash Bordeaux

KNEAD GLOP AND WAD.

Black pill. I force. Chew whole big pill dough, gawd ugh sweat

All right, horribleness

Ten minutes after gulp swallows, my stomach twists new. Like stomach has learned terrible fact.

Dr. Nobel's dark table. A hunk of ham and hunk of roast pork. Her son shreds at meats with big breadknife. He says he's creating "devil spread."

Meats end wrecked to snow bloody drifts. Then he stir combines in big glass bowl with wood-spoon blots of mayo. We taste his pinkish experiment with fingertips he stares his face aghast: he's invented accidental Spam!

He pretends barf. Then I pretend it. He can make me still laugh. But I *invented* it, he says, what if there was no such thing as Spam already? This would make me a TRILLION DOLLARS the first ever bowl of *sickening Spam*. And he's rest of lunch a tycoon, airplanes he'll fly between his Spam factories, Spam worker slaves waiting on his brow'll have-to-got-to bow down. I say And you'd eat Spam every day. *No I will not*, he says.

We are tycoons then, see our Monopoly tophats. We hire a secretary, we scream instructions at secretary Ko-Boo-Tah Piggy. She bows low hair flying, rushes to bring our demand. Idiot we won't fire her yet, we say, eating our Spam free lifetime supply. Long as she does her job she's safe from us.

Where are the important *contracts?* If the airplane leaves without us—slowly the mayo jar floats into air, airplanes tragically away. Piggy has failed to arrive with the *important contracts*.

Piggy shall pay.

We hold tycoon tribunal. Piggy stands before us. Look how much bigger we are. She tells us, admits, yes she's afraid. She's plastic quivering. Failed in her job, scared what we're going to do to her.

But (in boy's voice) you know what, she

says: I don't really care.

We look at her face.

I don't care about you, she says (my voice). Nothing you do to me can hurt, because I never have to be fake nice to you again.

Me and him look at each other.

We try being nice to Piggy. We say we won't hurt her. We don't hate you, we explain. We just got scared for our empire. See, when we're scared we *act* mean. Acting mean doesn't mean you're mean.

Piggy, with the boy's voice: So what does?

Can't stand this. Piggy hates us, I say.

She never liked us, says the boy.

Nobody to rule. Our empire dissolved. All we have left pink meat food we eat silent.

I'm waiting for him to cheer me up again. We never had this mood, just like my mood alone. I ruined him.

When Miss Nobel gets home the always change changes. Me and boy now can't see each other. His mother not mere boyfriend babysitter, life less like life (survived animals) more like love (family) she surrounds the red bumps on his neck and chest, she swamps his stomach hurt, his no appetite. I did notice he went sort've off, hoped it would just fix itself. "Shh—your head hurt any? does the light bother you? our voices sound weird at all?" She's overdoing the questions, I tell her calm down he's been *fine* all day, he can't be that sick don't worry. "You don't feel like dinner huh. Did you eat lunch?" *Of course he did* I'm saying, while she's saying "What *did* you eat?"

So able to diagnose simple Spam poisoning. Treatment pink bismuth in spoon, and he gets to sit with ginger tea while we eat dinner. No appetite me either, pluck at a corner of lasagna, me hear me still explaining *he* made the Spam, it was *his* idea. *Our lives are dry seaweed laid in a stupid line.* Boy jumpy watching me choke language, his spoon bangs edge of my plate while I'm trying to talk till his mother says hey enough percussion, stop. The boy suddenly looks right at her and lets out loudest I ever heard fart, immense.

Miss Nobel slaps her palms down on table actually yells "Now *look*—since when'd you turn into a *crazy slob? Who* you trying to impress?"

Upset whispers he couldn't help it, his stomach did it! Then runs out into the kitchen.

Oh I've ruined his personality forever.

She says "Incredible. All the people he has in him. You know feed him enough candy he turns into this bitter weak-headed geezer. Ever see that?" I didn't give him any candy, I say, *she stands up suddenly.*

What, I say.

She walks slow to the kitchen, calling him, I follow saying what *what*, relax he's OK. He's not in kitchen, she heads through to the garage, he's not in garage. But directly to back of garage, *deep-freeze.* She opens the big white lid! Her son looks up at her from lying in there, stretched atop the legs of lamb. Banged lid shut over himself but she heard it.

"To thaw out," he's saying, "when you're dead, in future when everybody likes me."

Miss Nobel grabs him up and hugs. I'm saying OK, it's OK, what's the matter, he's all right, he's not hurt at all.

"And if he was," muffled in his shoulder.

"Then we'd handle that, don't worry."

"And if suffocated," she says, "if I hadn't heard him, if frozen dead. We'd *handle that?*"

She carries him to the diningroom, lays him right out on table amidst dinner, he's playing FROZE-STIFF. *How do we thaw him out* she says, and frozen corpse jaw croaks "Birthday." After a second she goes gets box of sparklers—she lights one and puts it in his ice-statue hand. He peers at it. Lights go out. Red sparks fly across his chest, glide along table polish wood and fall off into night, red sparks right into boy's face, sparks pouring into plate of black lasagna! Boy, melting, illumines by hitting it with cold sparks pouring jagged red his mother's closed-eyes face.

I thought he was asleep in his room he in bed calls out to me walking past "So is farting a *mistake.* Are you supposed to do something else instead?"

"I think they want you to fart silent. So you pretend to act perfect that way."

"Oh. You sit there. And smile—"

"—yeah never admit. That's the rule I think."

"You wouldn't *smell* perfect."

I look at him, loud as I can manage I fart. I can see him dim face dark quilt trying to do same, but now it won't work.

She's playing Bach record I'm saying I hate, Bach so machine cold, she says she doesn't like it either it scares her. Anyhow we leave it going, me catching German phrases lyrics: man sings

Wenn alles sich zur letzen Zeit entsetzet

When everything arrives at the last second

Und wenn ein kalter Todesschweiß die schon erstarrten Gleider netzet

And when a cold death-sweat covers my stiff corpse and the crowded busy jammed-up music cycles rotates gives me all the time in the world to translate

"You're having a panic attack."

"*No* don't call it that. Why shouldn't I feel like this? Death is real. Somebody working on me from outside. Doll toy of me, they're attacking its stomach, no its chest."

She holds me, in her Bach coffinwood livingroom.

"You don't understand," I say, "this is normal."

She holds me. Saying stuff. Saying "He really loves you I think. He's never been this close to anybody but his father." I'm all Bach sweat, brain harpsichord clink-clink-clink.

She saying stuff, "I really would like a picture of us. Of you, of all three of us. I know you don't do *snapshots*, but couldn't you make some art about us?"

The German man's singing Jesus will make it all all right (DEATH).

"Usually don't do...happy pictures. Usually attack, make people look awful. Kill them. That's my *style*. Source of strength, so. So naturally I don't want to photograph you that way."

Still holding on, "Oh...naturally not. In that case."

"Hold on to me," she says. A black sparkler where each spark pours out a piece of black.

So now Albion's going to sit on my floor and tell me something he's never told anybody.

You don't have to do that, I say.

"There are connections between people," says Albion. He's drawing a diagram box in center named *Gwenna* lines coming out from this symbol. She's been one year dead, this week the anniversary.

Yeah I know, I say.

He's upset. He's using the word Moral some funny way. Gwenna left him—well he *threw her out*—she returned to her former boy. And that boy killed her. Yes I *know*, I say.

Albion explaining something not exactly Gwenna. He again reads out loud his Planning Outline dinnerwork in progress performance art. The first draft he'd already performed me the same way. That was the reading where I glanced into next kitchen while Albion roared and I saw torso David his head in the oven. I ran in, but David alive was just drawing pictures on inside oven walls. Humming long low resonant notes in there to drown Albion's rationalizing voice. David waved his nice hand to me but wouldn't come out of the oven.

I say now: it's really-good

If I were more sensitive he would not now have to tell me a *secret*.

I frustrate him. Gwenna's deadness same problem somehow as my slow wit.

He has a *video* of her *murder*, he says.

Because I can't put these words together, I wait.

Sure, because the nut, the nut boy who murdered her, weird bastard he killed her deliberately. *Cold*. He didn't even get overwhelm anger against her like Albion sometimes admittedly did. No he killed her without human feelings, *that* is inexcusable, and he documented it. Killed her with video documentation.

Everything Albion says about the boyfriend I see clearest. I look just like the nut boyfriend, so I still miss the point, "What was his name?"

"His name, Jim, was FUCK HIM."

Newspaper front-page story *Candyland Bee*

claimed this so-called boyfriend, despondent in motel, threatened in Gwenna's presence to kill himself—she saintly tried to grab shotgun to save him, *accident*—when he pulled trigger both died. Him lying on bed, her beside on floor. [Picture FOR INSTANCE me shooting Dinah in a newspaper photo. No accident no suicide, aim right at her head.] "Were *you* mentioned, in the newspaper?"

But according to videotape (according to Albion) went like this:

You see son-of-a-bitch black&white video boy lying on bed, propped head pillow. Bare chest caved-in pale longhair weedy whining at her and shouting, all can't make it out echo hollow cheap-video noise.

[silence of my kitchen hollows out, cheap]

Gwenna drifts into picture to muffled plead with him. A voice that does not carry. Doesn't seem her side-of-head, not how Albion remembered her side-of-head.

[no it's Dinah]

You see Weedy [his name, FUCK HIM, was Jim] reach down fetch up dark stick no, *gun* slant barrel gun down to nuzzle his own ear like phone listening. He is face without spirit. A beast could not hold this gun. She stops talk—you hear she's crying [making her cry, I've never heard this before, Dinah crying from me] then see him cant barrel angle away from his head just a couple inches, trick careful—*it goes off* smoke-spray she seems to jump out of frame [*oh no*]

He's dropped gun he's lying on the video bed. Actual life can end in gray video matter-spraying event. Is he dead? [am I justice dead?] Dead still dead video time runs on and on, video machine running in room of him dead [is Dinah dead?] she's *out of picture silent*. [is David dead?] is Gwenna dead? Three minutes he lies there no motion till you believe it, believe you have seen it. Suddenly wow he jumps up! and his face comes at the camera! End of videotape document.

> *soul operated camera*
> *my flesh killed my friend*
> *I have to bounce off motel walls forever* in life

she was dead and he was dead. In life newspaper funeral they were both found dead. Nobody to answer the question. Metal walls forever and my friends' kitchen dark is a metal wall, Albion is a metal wall: David alone in the dark. David walled-in. Every photograph slapped his face with his face. In life he dead and she. *It must be* that he jumped up, shut off camera and then. Then sank horror: I shot her. No then sank frustration I've shot her and need a re-take. My actress dead. Shall I take pictures of David's friend Dinah, make the coffin wide-angle dark and slant ironic? Close-up fascinating attitude leg and thorax for crawling on her grave bugs?

"I decided the guy was brilliant," declares Albion in his art-school metal wall. If they'd actually'd just died together *oh is Dinah dead too?* did I kill her? *was she fragile even more than David* if they'd simply bang and died on-camera then it's just television, video snuff. But this way. How does a metal wall bear it—a voice is only a vibration, words only noise, a bearded Albion face doesn't make a fat wall, recover yourself hey David my face doesn't make a wall, hey David my betrayal friend Jim face doesn't make a wall, David the roomful of photo lookers seeing you doesn't see you, if I can puncture through expanding Albion then Dinah and David you two can succeed escape [from me] and live.

But this was it's a Brecht idea he's working, Video Death for You Watchers—with death of the artist commented on yet included, under artistic control. Very unusual piece of work.

Was Dinah fragile even more than David—I trusted her! I trusted her version of her face that *never changes* it can't suffer. Hey Dinah come on bounce off metal wall *attack me:* reveal yourself! Like a *friend* "Albion—what you're telling me—is it true? Did this video exist really? Or you made that all up, to get your play-dinner more interesting?"

Metal wall his face glass-screen bland: *"That shouldn't make so much difference."*

About a minute later blood drains from behind my eyes. I sit on the floor.

"There are connections between people," he says.

He walking around my kitchen reads me from Paracelsus, antique asserter each food ingredient has its own *virtue*. What's a virtue? Seems people can communicate. By *eating* certain things.

Humans were meant to understand each other, sympathy is a model for this, I eat a burger and touch the burger in you. He's leaning against my enlarger, the dome of it right back of his head he looks alchemist, his beard down into his book like putting black powder in a flask of purple, I say because I can't think, gut too killing for subtle remark, what the fuck happened to your life? Why not move out from your father, meet a new girl— forget ART— Me and my father, he says. My father prevents every single thing. Check this out THE REASON WHY BULL'S FAT IS SO POWERFUL IS THAT THE BULL AT THE TIME OF SLAUGHTER IS FULL OF RELUCTANCY AND VINDICTIVE MURMURS, AND THEREFORE DIES WITH A HIGHER FLAME OF REVENGE ABOUT HIM THAN ANY OTHER ANIMAL. You know when somebody you love has a headache, and you get one too? That has a physiology. It's a real headache. Certain foods can make you hallucinate, or make you hyper-energetic, or make you die.

Is a real headache love? Poison. I think it's called chemistry.

Science is not so smart, he says. They see what they want to see, make up Latin for what won't fit. GASTRITIS. It means gut, hurts. That's the *meaning* of the word.

Are your dinners making you feel better? My pictures aren't curing me, my gut hurts all the time like I'm dying, I tell him, admit, confess.

What do you eat? How do you feel? Guilt

about stuff is for goofs! You are poisoning yourself, guilt to be turned *outward*. And reads to me more, very loud now, very bad.

I finally saw Gwenna die. Can't listen to Paracelsus supposed to fix it! *Can't listen to this shit.* My stomach sees David's stomach lying across his spine on a lawn chair somewhere, how his feels, I never realized: his must hurt all the time. Our stomachs talking to each other.

My stomach screws tight suddenly, seeing this very man Albion kissing at Gwenna's living mouth, sucking her mouth at the front of her living skull. Her skull got turned outward. Behind my eyes starts pounding, salt taste in mouth, *science symptom* pounding heart, fear just OK medical panic but I think Gwenna's head, her head is talking to mine, her embalming fluid coming up my throat/////

Brain head dark liquid.

Oh bad. Every soul ever dead now having sympathy suck.

My brain head, dark, liquid. I'm alone on the black wobbling plate. I'm alone above my lost throat, out of balance hit the floor in the gut center of Albion fat throat voice.

Albion is just a dark liquid.

Then in another time Albion dark liquid trying to take me by the body. Hoist drag me along down steps steps down steps tanker slosh oil through canal locks soup sidewalk down slop liquid inner vessel slurp roll down. Has thrummed words liquid often *emergency room* sound sludge.

Then very clear a second at street I see him whistle a box with no connection to him, and box connects, taxi. Feel of the vinyl door-hold's the way flesh doesn't stop existing after flesh's died. You're still there, in the back seat, leaning on the door. It's just that because dead, people say: meat

Thank you. He is being friend, emergency room. Albion the son of Chef beloved of Gwenna true friend to Jim, Jim balanced in chair, Jim promised life survival future, Albion voice booming kindly connecting entire Candyland emergency room reading me for friend company his ancient book. A GENTLEMAN AT BRUSSELS HAD HIS NOSE MOWED OFF IN A COMBAT, BUT THE CELEBRATED SURGEON TAGLIACOZZUS DIGGED A NEW NOSE FOR HIM OUT OF THE SKIN OF THE ARM OF A PORTER AT BOLOGNA. ABOUT THIRTEEN MONTHS AFTER HIS RETURN TO HIS OWN COUNTRY, THE ENGRAFTED NOSE GREW COLD, PUTREFIED, AND IN A FEW DAYS DROPPED OFF

now my whole world one little aisle plastic molded turquoise chairs, man demonstrating broken section of hispanic leg cast removable and beneath white green fungus-fuzzy stick shriveled leg

AND IT WAS THEN DISCOVERED THAT THE PORTER HAD EXPIRED, NEAR ABOUT THE SAME PUNCTILIO OF TIME

woman tight white hair leaning back on one gripping arm a whole black terrycloth towel held to her eyes covers her face, I never do see a face, her body doesn't move

matbearded man holds mouth open he's kneeling on the floor in front of his turquoise plastic chair, ignored by the serene young man beside, he holds his mouth, holds, then silently vomits into a strange red cloth bag the size of his head, and reappears holding dark mouth open, rocking back and forth

woman with long upper lip no chin nobility set of head holds silent baby in one arm and crying hairless dog in other

none of us can listen to Albion's book

woman with black towel her husband's inside been after 40 years married hit by a refrigerated delivery truck because the driver had to hurry up

man with red cloth bag has been fed by a kind stranger street food consisting pork and glass and beans

woman with baby and dog dares not leave them

alone with her husband who has this evening
broken the bone behind her left ear

young man serene came on errand of mercy help
cheer up young woman who overdosed under his
tutelage

Beneath my eyes now a muscle black foot,
toes pointing right at me. Other foot out angle,
muscle thick calves sway a little, feet grip the linoleum. Hercules with bent head looking at the floor
beard mustache eyebrows concentrating. He's
holding a whole man upright in the air, man as big
as he hugged to his chest, together they're eight feet
tall. Hercules side of head supports chest of other
man, neck muscles rope, one arm waist grapple,
other hand protective wrapped nape. The man in
air relaxed like complete deep dangling sleep on
rock hanging over cliff, the back of him white
T-shirt chocolate-dark blood, blood all the held
man's legs, blood in the holding man's beard, blood
his diluting-sweat face and chest, blood down his
own legs, sticky under his gripping feet. He just
looking down waits. He won't let stone-block huge
true friend touch the ground.

I PRAY WHAT IS THERE IN THIS OF
SUPERSTITION OR OF EXALTED IMAGINA-
TION? glue Albion voice still proving me something. But Gwenna's face is my face. My stone face
grows cold, putrefies, drops off. My face is David's
face. I can't lift my arms. Stomach muscles rigid

final increase now of usual pain. Weak too much to shift in chair. Eyes are work to focus, but glimmer *happy* to see the held-high man finally lowered to white gurney and rolled beyond.

Police gripping Hercules, they're taking a box-cutter blade from his back pocket. His wet face is tired, meek.

Banging noise.

Banging on empty oildrum.

Everybody's higher-up than me.

Somebody says: *I am going to die right here.*

They celebrate. They pound something empty.

I see the ceiling. Ceiling lights sprocket rolling up.

Elevator tomb.

Soft. Oh I'm lying down.

Later: a lamp with strangled neck. Instead of light it puts out food, clear bulb of liquid ideal sterile food.

Later, breath of a kind man. Turquoise toy-color plastic duct and needle he makes part of my arm, his breath saying the word *feel.*

Then TELEVISION. I'm warm. She says roll over on your side. I'm happy.

I see fingers. Her face is Miss Nobel.

My actual Miss Nobel here taking my nose into her fingertips. See her and I don't even feel tense pang. Big snowscreen TV set right beside her face. I haven't spoken to her.

Snuffle, she says, sniff, relax.

Tube down I realize my left nostril swordswallower try to relax, down my throat she says *camera tiny light probe.*

And her sex fingers have rubber gloves feed guide the black tube.

When nostrils flare. When she touches delicate my bare flesh nose.

She's entering my nose but face turned away, she's watching the TV.

On the huge color TV is my tunnel, cop searchlight motion forward down red and yellow-white tunnels into black zone, dammed-pressure source of all black misery fountain, the black air black liquid search for any integument, squishy horror blue vein-grimace walls and black shit, lake of shit, lake bag black soup and me not even a machine I'm a growth.

Where is her face. I need to check. I jerk my nose away from her hand.

Her face appears. All I see is lower lip pressed up hard against upper little teeth. Not a smile.

Even aswim in drug casserole I hurt to see her face now that she's seen me.

My insides on videotape. If ever thinks I'm beautiful she can check the tape.

Now that she's seen this.

You leave a woman so you can start clean. "New" woman never saw my bile duct like octopus nostril-flaring sex ingress dilating without my will. New woman untraumatized by my shitty innards.

She doesn't know, she believes in skin!

Woman you walk out on—relieved to watch your dirty ass go. Person betrayed says good now I can puke him out. You are being helpful to the people you hurt. Showing them truth, they appreciate that in the long run.

She looking down at my body in hospital bed, my woman looking down at my body, she's holding tiny little white pleated-paper cup hospital Maalox chalk liquid between fingertips, whole time she speaks it hovering dead still far above my face, so my whole body tense against the spillage of dead chalk liquid down on my face, tense like that would be terrible signal for commence death-spell against me, tension slowly becoming same thing as fever, tense and fever wheel counterclock together, hard for me to listen while, not disputing science with me (because into the mouth of her gentle flowing medical jargon I repeat insist somebody's holding a voodoo doll image against me, I can see pale little image its blue gown), she only tells a doll story—I don't know it's only a doll story—if she doesn't spill Maalox slop chalk-mark white face then it's only a doll story—she's been awhile talking I'm already missing the point—her saying her son had never saved up money to buy a thing before, very healthy for him *word (HEALTHY) makes impossible to concentrate* but I do fever see what's really just words when words're injected in fever tense muscle-relaxant IV-heat floppiness stone-seizure stomach and Maalox damocles: picture, here's her son in a toystore. I'm glad to see him.

What he wants is doll called GI JOE. GI Joe has scary close-up *huge orange face.* Square nose block head, this hurts. I grip on watching of kid, try to hear what he's saying because I'm all slack, what should be never relaxed is. I gather: boy's been thinking wanting this doll toy for weeks, *Who made this* I ask. Boy's voice: "Who? Hasbro. Made by Hasbro." Toystore human-shape armorplate light-blink killers piled in stacks on the shelf, *Who made this?* "Ideal," he says kneeling flipping through twenty identical GI Joe doll cardboard cello-window display boxes. He looks twenty times the words on boxes all printed same colors and flips through watching same exclamation point go past! looks exciting each time! *can't* be. So maybe wants one identical Joe that's not here—do they have any more? Or wants to buy them all up, ARMY, own every Joe ever made so you can do what you imagined feeling doing, you want to *own GI Joe.*

Finally buying one, no pretend it's not "one" it's *it,* try to have excitement buying IT. Money he saved up they want him to pay down. He wants to keep money and also have the Joe. Relinquish. Now he's lost his money and the weeks of thinking about and all nineteen Joes possible, all he owns is this doll here. Finally *owns,* Joe is *his* he tries to remember anticipation happy Joe. In car he has it march, it's supposed to do that, then he drops soldier stuff it's just Joe doll Joe, it can fly it can go.

Somehow not a very good doll. Big, too

stupid. On its third day of life boy slides it out slot bedroom window. Fallen Joe can't breathe stunned head-down dirt under jungle hedge. Ex-owner strolls around house without Joe...Joe gone lost...no more doll...wanders accidentally outside, "finds"...thrill he owns Joe again.

He doesn't want it. Wants to keep *buying* it.

Starts to test doll against other objects. Books he likes can fall on and kill it. His gyroscope poke into Joe's eye cause blindness. Doll weaker than anything. Doll just dumb. Can't get your money back.

With copper penny heated in tongs stove flame red-hot boy is burning face of doll. Joe inexpression flattens black plastic smoke.

Doll just a thing you use. Doll a weight to stick on erector-set motorized smasho machine so machine heavy enough swing its arm smash.

Doll ends high in the air face burnt off, wrapped dead mummy in whole ball of kitestring, only bare feet and blot face head showing. Doll balanced upon Great Ledge of GI JOE SCIENCE PAVILION MEMORIAL takes up whole center of bedroom, six feet tall tower lego lincoln-log erector-set tinkertoy, the top is slab Great Ledge hanging there impossible, against gravity, a whole yard long polyglot toy matter suspended in air cause he's got it hanging from the ceiling light by secret plastic *indivisible threads*, and stuck out at far edge no-gravity Mummy Joe.

Dream trace my floating eye now backward

from Joe to ledge to fat round toy building gets smaller and smaller toward the floor, and at very floor is just one orange tinkertoy rod on end, and into the tip wood's forced a *pin*. Guy-wire thread grapple everyplace holding all up, building enormity resting on the head of pin. Whole must weigh 30 pounds, kid's kneeling looking at that pin, decides head of pin too fat easy, wants to turn the pin around, wants all balanced on *point* pin, but this late daunting to revise—here face to face his mother recognizes the mummy. She's shocked; he only bought Joe last week.

No, he says: this is to show him off.

No, he says, I *like* him. He's easier to *see* up there.

How did she save my life. She made me so nothing was invisible.

Her hands clicking keyboard. Keys sweep dirty radar windshields. Radar drives into discovery storms of blob. She opens my blob insides on sheets of film sonar.

Her hands clicking keys, dips my entire body cotton wrapped into magnetic resonance, plastic airline coffin beige soft lighting and her voice on loudspeaker *Breathe. Don't breathe. Breathe* photos of my upper body sheets of film cross-section by dozens like all you can eat roll sushi.

Nothing is not visible. All information already exists, isn't any knowledge we lack. Problem is accessing CLICK CLICK CLICK

CLICK
CLICK
CLICK

Can you call up meaning info on:
this conversation we're having now
Someplace an expert on everything about me. Knows totally more than me about my life, how to make it go. It's in a book text at end of modem, already been worked up by specialists.

Can you translate:
the way you rubbed your eyes just then, and looked defeated
Oculist database   searching
Checked me out of hospital us both hoping I'd take my skin bag shit soup and slog it to house not hers. Till my skin grow opaque sex-colored again.

Try cheer up sit alive in my kitchen wait for my skin. Make up some pictures out of nothing.
Basketball stolen/found among presumed abandoned junk of presumed ex-friends
Found-art, that's "found" mind you

"Art of appropriation" they say "making the viewer complicit"

Uh: a basketball wearing a hat.

Basketball turned from *nothing*, thing primitive people used for "play," into *art photo*

Dinah's basketball wearing a hat: hat found/ appropriated from off David's turned-away head dark blue w/gold latitude cubscout visor piping cap

Orange pimpled face with swirl black lines and Voit words where mouth is. Lines of ball lines of cap, these are formal. All the lighting in the world this'll never be a good photograph. Good means somebody likes it who isn't me. Only I would get it about this hatted face who'll never speak.

I can't how-to-take-pictures can't what-they're-for.

I steal their packet snapshots found forgot under their newspapers and their dust.

Is this how?

Snapshot privacy: Dinah says to David: I see you playing skee-ball at Atlantic City. I remember your fingers on the wood ball and gentle concentration. Afterwards I had to show you machine'd been keeping score.

Privacy I overhear: David says to Dinah: I see you on the bench when it's not important, remember you beside me when nothing is memorable. Your face in dimension realer than cloud sky, this thing I need, what I need not draw, could never draw well as it draws itself.

Dinah: We were on the road in snowstorm,

car broken, you clearing off windshield made your green shirt flag you center of the world against all white and black.

David: You at very center my fear of huge Mexican cliff wall. I can parody compose fine pictures here and here and here, but with you within picture you're center the whole of it, nothing balances you off. And we ate the 45¢ breakfast and lived heat of day on battered many-times refilled greenglass bottles of Mexican Squirt. Me being in terror partly from making you unhappy with my terror, would I hurt lose you, but here you laughing at the center of the rock, EVIDENCE. I was happy making you happy.

Are they just snapshots? Pictures can't be less strong than they look. I can't learn anything from these they're distorted by love.

Letter envelope to *James* Chapman doesn't say Dear Jim, not signed at bottom. No return name address.

"I am trying to piece together the disintegration. I criticized your photography. Unfair. I saw how upset that made you.

"When I feel guilty I try to fix it. I try to pay with something real. So I told you things I've never told anybody. Story about David's breakdown in Mexico and the scary car trip back to L.A., awake

48 hours, the things I felt, the things I was forced to do. You were a good friend, you listened and tried to get me feeling it was just a *story*.

"When you started taking pictures of us every night, I thought of it as your private goodness. You were recording us to give me a way to see life as ongoing. Cause you knew I was about to snap, fear, protecting David-and-me from David. Pretty soon you handed me an envelope of photographs you were calling 'Dwarf Maple: A Photo Essay.'

"You told me it was *all about David's break-down.*

"I protect. I hid it from him. Never looked at it myself. I protect! Later you told me I *better* look at the pictures because you were going to try to publish them in a magazine.

"Finally David asked me what was going on between you and me. I had to tell him. He suffered a relapse, overnight in the hospital, drugs, the psychiatrist, I know, I'm supposed to be strong, steady, calm. For David's sake I act like passer-of-all-tests. I make a stable world for him. *You are setting me new tests.*"

That letter instead of breakfast.

Noon I drink bottle mineral water at the restaurant downstairs.

Then spoon black soup tail of ox.

Slices of dark bread, plant salad, I leave the restaurant.

That was lunch, *hold me* till dinner.

Walk up street downtown Clavis Hotel

lobby lounge sit order eat a MEDLEY slice pork sausages stalk celery; guess I was still hungry.

Washed down with unlabeled white wine split.

Then small blot custard then slice strawberry ice-cream-cake.

Now really wellfed walk along Astartis Road to inside linoleum bus station.

There I do have two sections PB MAX machine candy also one machine Baby Ruth bar dessert, sit watch passengers decide Jersey towns and all leave, I sip machine-dribble whitener product coffee.

Bus station bar dark red rug drink one no ice John Haig Red Label.

Then request eventually receive small glass of prune juice.

JUMP on city bus land out at Candyland Plaza's French Riviera café *Magica* order but unable to eat dish called Pear Hélène.

In lieu a pear schnapps.

No farther walk exercise other end of mall find fry plate grease Chicken Strips after that a huge pile Shaved Beef.

I eat all then order Pork Twirls. Waitress attempts speak to me.

Two p.m. the plate arrives.

Plate sits still, piled up entangled, Pork Twirls.

Hey, answer me.

Miss Nobel won't. Talks on:

You aren't dying. Change your life. Normal balanced diet, relaxing environment, reduce stressful conflicts, eat with no haste.

What about what I just said?

I hear you swallowing air. Common in neurotic patients, Jim. Swallowing air leads to flatulence, Jim.

I feel fine. I'm not an object!

...eventually causing scentless farts. The patient is trying to live on air. Scentless farts because nothing can come of nothing. You dry up, the whole system starts to stop.

How come I've never seen you cry over a patient?

Because you never have seen me cry over a patient. Because now I cry outside the trap of patients. I can't handle it, so. So I cry about the door, I look at the elevator door and cry. I cry because there's light shining through an ugly dressing gown hanging on a spike.

Medical profession. That's why you don't have a lot of compassion. People are just things to repair.

I've cried about you.

Do you touch the breast button on your camera like compassion?

I've cried because of you. Not *over* you, but due to you. My son loves you. Are your symptoms terrible? Is that what turns you into this creep? My son loves you, Jim.

I'll never photograph you. You're...too sacred to me.

As long as you talk like a shit, the result's some form of truthfulness, is that right?

I don't know. I haven't worked it out yet.

Well, you're not young.

Dinah in tiny, dozens Dinah. Every contact sheet the rows little faces like pale bugs twisting escape from parallel lines of sprocket frame edge. Hundreds Davids Dinahs rejected version faces. One of each 36 cruel enough to print. Cruel I was calling Strong.

Hundreds of these. Now they look different.

Developer ripples tray yellow light. No more roommates so work all night if I want.

Sweat drip cutting up all proofsheets little postagestamp pictures into face life. To see moments alone.

Lying on the floor dim staring one tiny slip of paper Dinah eyes closed smiling pressing her hands together.

On wall above enlarger the main picture on my wall: Lazarus climbs out cave gold leaf.

Lazarus face dead awe toward finger of Jesus. Jesus in red robe looking at us bland, this is easy for him.

I tape tiny Dinah over his face. Inhale, arms around my stomach

squeeze inhale more

squeeze harder inhale more

And pictures I did print. Vicious knowing little *captions* comments.

Developer smell kills all food.

Reprint re-caption.

Dinah *Fragile*

Dinah and David, her mouth speaks *Go talk to Jim*

Dinah and David, her mouth looks at camera *Betray me*

Dinah *I feel nothing yet*

David *Ill*

David *Who wants to hurt me, please do not*

These captions very INEFFECTIVE. I flex fingers in the dark, try strength of being INEFFECTIVE.

Dinah *David's not here*

(If I run into him on the street he'll *scream*. Don't yell back at him don't hurt him. He's right he's screaming at me.)

Dinah *You couldn't have me so tried to kill him*

New captions not good at all.

David: no caption. Darkened prey having to walk through room where I sit with my camera. (I knew this)

Dinah: no caption. Mouth open pressure, terrible young upset face. (I noticed)

Dinah: looking at me. No words.

David: looking at me. No words.

Dinah and David on sofa, legs tangled.
Calm.

No caption there either

Is it necessary to have pictures

No picture: David dead. Now today dead someplace. Why else haven't I heard from them?

David eyes shut: *Why else*

Grainy David, not a picture. David white gray floating, no picture. David flat silent.

Opens eyes right at me.

Fades up from flat white bedsheet, speaks without voice, without his freckled throat:

What do you want

Now he's cut loose now lost wandering now he's dead

Then if I see his picture: a dead guy laughing looking at me sees nothing.

My mouth open. Chest can't suck. Stomach burbling stone.

Again lie awake poor me.

Switch on light I look at his picture again. Same. Light dark.

Hour later check it again. This a vertical picture. Turn it on its side. David sideways sliding. David escaping in, or out.

Then do sleep some.

Light of the moon my stuffed head wan woozy silver, why my kitchen floor am I awake? suddenly feet walking past my eyes mattress. David silver face small in corridor flicker, blink he's gone.

I could sleep. A second chance with my friends, a chance to be good be loved: I could sleep through it. Give my dreams the chance. Suddenly very sleepy. That might be best. Do less.

Too hungry to sleep.

They're in their kitchen, I can't see them. Domestic small noises again.

Too hungry to sleep. *Starving*. The zucchini looks black in the moon. I get up chop at it, it's silver inside, the knife black-silver.

Don't want to confront them or don't want to be confronted don't wish to disturb or

Nobody could draw this moon zucchini. Only photo rescues silver light. Having David Dinah in the next room is my paralyzed starving stare whether to set up time exposure of food under my hands or to complete and devour omelette.

David touching my forearm.

I switch on the light and he shuts eyes with his whole face, flapping hands and I switch light off again.

Hug him, god it's good to see you again. Are you hungry?

Cook breakfast 4 a.m. zucchini omelettes for me and David in the dark, making our half-sentence whispers mesh together, assume for preference Dinah's asleep. Then whole chinese teapot of coffee, got his new drawings spread out all over the floor.

Because breakfast has a trick. These drawings he was never probably going to show me. I made him one omelette and he just gave over, handed me big envelope like letter him to me.

Heavy sheets vellum and drawing intricate so much crosshatch the ink soak wrinkles sheets *covers* paper brown ink. Brown ink antique pictureframes drawn detail squaring border each picture.

One monk cowl like Artaud face directing dozens of naked workers haul buckets up dug-out pit hell. Little drawn brass plaque reads *The Gold Diggers*.

One priest goatee Ezra Pound holding riding-crop his hundreds of brown ink workers faces in dirt, in nearest low corner a worker eating the dirt, *Dredgers Worship True Work*.

Pope in sedan chair so fat fat spilling on ground, men holding him aloft are all huge legs strain, heads bent away. Pope face beauty like Lord Byron. *Arbeit Macht Frei*.

Severe religious terror order fourteen drawings spread out on my floor, me examine each in the dark shine beam down from my big black metal flashlight I bought next-door to Candyland police academy.

Watching, but without shining beam in it, David's face.

No camera because too dark, but memorize the photographs I'm losing: David's slouch into hands on face, his body drown mid-sea of his own drawings, his trusting stare up mighty walls of my own image clutter, his gaze down into my circle of cop light like into bright burning poison well. Hard seeing him not to speak captions.

They're very "good" I tell him. I pull them all together in little categories this pile and that, explaining, then pile them all together and stack tap loud on floor, slide back in envelope talking, I demonstrate my mind by referring many dif images while not even looking, I *needn't look again.*

Then for his own good, I begin attack: why you change into this orderly drawing caution? Why you drawing on rectangles of paper now, and composing balancing? That interests me less than the work you used to be able to do, the freer work. I bet Dinah told you try these commercial forms. I bet she felt it'd do you good, she really I find prefers conventional art. Perhaps you're scared these days to let loose, maybe that worries you. Me I always'm cheered up by very wild art, it seems hopeful even if it drives other people nuts. Some artists die away *had potential* but *became boring.* Oh I know what! You want the world to find you NORMAL. Normal guy making sane OK pictures. Maybe feeling sane's important to you. Even *somehow* more important than doing *great work.* All right let's accept that. I get frustrated cause you're capable of great mastery if you'd just cut loose from your life.

David nodding eyes at the corners of my body not speaking. No camera too dark. I memorize pictures David obliqued, but get desperate: these pictures lost. I can't take them later on. What goes goes gone into mere life.

Would it bother him too much I wonder, flash pictures? Dinah's face suddenly in dark above our dirty dishes, moon, wistful Dinah love fills me, hey hi I hug her, I make knowing mouth wry eyes. She's *fine* willing to sit with us *fine* no problem—sits says immediately listen David c'mon. We got to sleep.

But me talking on about his drawings again, now I'm gonna impress her too, exhaust them proof logic they both should love admire me, and even while I'm talk talking hung too far out on rosary logic string to not complete my speech, Dinah's looking into David's face. Her mouth despite me making words no sound words. Two inches from David's face, her fingers on his cheeks in the dark. Mouthing into his pale face very slow

$$\begin{pmatrix} \text{You} & \text{are} & \text{OK} \\ \text{I} & \text{am} & \text{here} \\ \text{I} & \text{love} & \text{you} \\ \text{We} & \text{are} & \text{fine} \\ \text{Don't} & & \text{worry} \end{pmatrix}$$

deflates effect of my analysis.

Inside the envelope David's drawings silent. No matter I rail against shape of paper they're drawn on, in dark envelope drawings haven't changed. I could throw them out window into the wind and they'd fly around city being just as good. They're very good. "They're very *good*" I allow, then can't stand it:

"Oh, you guys want to go to a club tomorrow night? It's like a poetry reading and they're going to have some *slides too*, I made slides out of those pictures."

Dinah doesn't say What pictures.

"Those pictures I took of you guys, they're going to project them, it'll be just small crowd there. And David listen maybe I could show these drawings to the woman who's running the series, I'm sure she'd be interested." Because of what a nice guy I am, David can't budge his face.

Dinah says it:

"Uh—I don't think so, Jim." Sarcastic, "Uh—*no*..."

No camera to put in front of my face.

(David draw all the pictures of me you want. Show me how I am. Attack me, I can take it I can take it why can't you? Humiliation wouldn't be anything much!)

You can see in the dark, says David to me.

You don't *understand*, he says to me.

He shakes Dinah off him, puts his face right in my eyes. And I *see* his face. Hollow-dark green eyes puffed medication eye-bags, stubble gapes around mouth, cheeks wet, all gray dark.

I DISENCHANT you don't I? he says. You pick me up, grub grub pick click you dis—DISINTER. Something you don't know about my shit horrible drawing: always I change *one line*.

(Dinah saying davidavidavidavid)

Even if I make a picture of you someday.

Even if I put up a huge painting of you. Out on the highway. So every pig fuck with a can of beer can drink up and drive out there to piss on you. And write big JIM CHAPMAN right where the piss hits *even then*—it won't hurt you. Cause it won't BE YOU. I always change one line, I draw one line different. So it's not you they piss all over. I make sure it's *me*.

Dinah pulls David with her gone.

Gone, how I feel doesn't matter. He is the one who needs to be able to sleep.

David has to sleep.

David has to sleep now. His dark pitch tremor hands. Kneels up on mattress because his heartbeat jumped. His hands black gone flat unable find mattress beneath him a thousand black miles.

And remembers own body, sucks in sudden air.

Gulps air

David hungry for air

sucking puffing

blue light in eyes

prickles in forehead

Drops through space tingling fingers open out slow falls on his side.

Not breathing.

Dark is far. He hears me. Far across the dark, he hears sound of another thing sucking air, gasp blow gulps.

It doesn't matter, how I feel. Because I'll live.

Daylight. It's dead quiet in the other kitchen that's woke me.

Alone gone again. Carried out rest of their personal junk. Whole block of presence now air. Life simplified. Whole weight empty.

Dr. Nobel's office, close my eyes, turn head away dark, then back to her voice. Open my eyes a quarter-second and shut them again. In my black eyelids her face stop, mouth half-open, hand gesture deformed, her eyes down at desk thoughts on her thoughts. This woman the photographer loved during the period of his illness.

Her head against black would make hair glow out. More glow baby spot on hair and two main lights model face. Now: open eyes for a blink moment/close. Openblink/close. Again thirty times more, one of these silent the woman you might prefer.

Light into my face, Dr. Nobel says "Grimace. Scrunch up your face and hold it. Like," she makes her face pain.

Full light glare I make her a tortured face. She's examining slowly, slowly, to see if I'm lopsided neurologically. Wrinkles on one side of face not other, hair going gray one temple only, headaches in back of one eye? Looking straight into my scrunched left side face with her unified gaze, then into right.

So. How come you never take any self-portraits? You want to be remembered I thought.

Oh I hate having my picture taken.

I've never seen *any*, she says, not even kid pictures. I bet you were cute, what did you look like?

There aren't any pictures. I just looked like myself.

Well I doubt that.

Albion mutters me to have fun and alone I stand up.

Audience eyes say I'm one of them. They direct me to lower my eyes lectern and smile.

Forty people watching me, the self-reading-poet community assets of scene Candyland. They tell me support the arts by starting *now* don't out-stay our welcome, leave us wanting.

The room painted performance-space black and black cloth over the door in the back. Cloth moves black on black moves. David comes in, sits immediate down all the way in back nearest escape door table.

He doesn't give direction.

Forty people say *come on* hey we know movie entertainment timing, *cut!*

Light dim lectern light I click my slide-projector wand but there is nothing. No slide projected to take over my face. Caught

Girl in back fumbling in my name with carousel plastic projector time time *caught* at a *loss*

Should speak clever, silence and blame approach from all space like dust.

Caught must hide my face, bring from belt-clip my little camera and photograph the murky crowd

which act of mine they laugh approvingly adore me for

feels *wonderful.*

The first slide click DAVID HUGE

I think of looking for David's living face in back, but the crowd does not direct me to do so, there's no time, there's no freedom I'm *busy.*

David huge black&white sucking a cigarette staring at his bare foot like flesh gray tomb he burns incense.

I microphone read to all my new friends the revised caption, the de-fanged. *"Please don't look at me."* My voice rings too loud amplified-weakness slashes me electronic stupid: this new caption LAME AND FLAT. Old rejected caption went "My foot deserves to die," old caption would have worked! A flop I sweat flop into annoyed forty important people silence annoyed at me so hard I have to hide photograph them again though they're too dim, only photographable'd be my lit-up face hiding behind camera, this now old trick wins no approval noise. Makes worse, sweat worse, they are about to direct me disappear.

Thump click next slide. I never notice switching from notecard to memory old original caption, David's flat close-up partly closed eyes

Stoic. Punctured bladder

better mike-adjust voice modulates quiet deep, they've directed me well and I'm homing in on them. Now the silence is better, stiller. And each picture comes through

Bent worm dead of filthy light
Heedless slave of my own zombie eyes
All smiles, laughingstock!

on the original harsh caption plan, my voice can even shout act, silence now actually rapt, *I direct*. Great pleasure glow.

And with skimp part mind I'm also watching dim audience event:

along the left wall:

audience girl dim turns away from me:

she's turned entirely around to check and it's true,

staring at David at his little back table

then still looking grabs at wrist of her boyfriend. This makes the table behind them do the same look.

All the way in the back one little person stands up fast walks out the door. David

Albion at front table right now takes flash polaroid of me blinding out the whole darkness.

(Later I look at this polaroid: me serious commanding.)

No space in mind to picture David running down the street

Obviously must finish this performance, professional cannot quit dash out after him. Work through this distraction rebuild strength. Forty people depending on me.

Within a few click slides get my voice timing back, fight away image David throwing self down sewer no me me: brave dramatic continue perform into even such disturbance, what theatre power talent.

Stone

Stone close-up stone silence

Applause: APPLAUSE!   *if this could be permanent*

I make it back through food applause quench applause to our table, our table seems glowing up, Albion very cool, not looking at me, does grip my elbow a second under the table, wow everything glorious, forget David now got to stay for Albion reading, loyal I owe this night all to him. David alive and well I'm *sure*. All he was a walk-out. Wish he'd stayed. It was good, even he'd admit. He may've liked it more than he could bear. He's just shy. Not like me.

(Miss Nobel was unable to attend.)

Of course Albion ends showing us all how

it's really done: his bulk beard voice booming out shockwaves from forehead to belly *portrays* Gwenna, does the voices, raw words world's screaming at innocent Gwenna, horrible raw words for desire. Parodies self at castrato pitch artiste simplex, then operatic bursting poems by the murderer beast, he lights Sterno tab and burns blobs of animal fat on a rust tin tong-held shingle square, flesh stink smells *good* as he as chorus street-people rants shrieks phrases of possession. Albion even dances his surprise graceful huge self the dance of shotgun around her (her = empty space he creates). Throws flowers in the wet fat smoke. And wafers of crushed god flesh crumbs flung at audience in his final self-hate prayer shoutings.

Applause yelling cheering! Albion sits back down, at *my* table, putting audience eyes back on *me* friend-of-Albion insider, but I'm not clapping, I'm stunned. His face dark red grabs my shoulder violent traps little table base in his thighs and rocks it, squeezing it all into his crotch, low harsh whisper at side of my head, *I got 'em!*

Me not clapping. Because still with Gwenna forget my sociable face.

With Gwenna, she's under the covers.

I'm lying atop covers, a bed in front of an audience. Gwenna still, maybe asleep. Because I have to try explain one thing more. Run hand across my mouth, my hand's flaking-off blood. Blood smear adhesions to face hands arms, put forearms over my eyes. Microphone shh don't wake her. Ka-tick, tick—new slide projection on wall behind our bed. Newsphoto piles of bodies. Ka-tick, tick six alive skeleton men about-to-die liberated. Audience silent ice so I can speak thinking. Holocaust photos, I whisper to microphone, shot by famous *Life Mag* woman Margaret Bourke-White. Anonymous-looking, aren't they. She rejected them, they lack her personal style. Can't look at any of these and go Oh that's Margaret Bourke-White.

Ka-tick but see *this* picture is greatness: row of men standing, all OK healthy, none starving, soft lighting from the left side, blackness behind, men hold on to fence, fence makes beautiful line, see how striped trousers on this one man makes other beautiful line. Solemn faces big dark eyes. They've seen something we are not being forced to see. Beauty men standing *obstructing* the death camp behind them. This famous picture we appreciate. You see how many we have to throw away before we get one we can use. Sometimes throw out thousands. Single great one worth all the rest combined.

Gwenna pulls covers over her head.

Ka-tick *My kitchen floor covered blood.*

Ka-tick *In restaurant freezer hanging half-a-cow.*

Ka-tick *Wood kitchen floor all spatters fat trims vegetable pares mash clot potato, beet juice.*

Ka-tick *Gwenna's smiling, body naked spattered shredded beets.*

Ka-tick *David lying on his back, trying not to breathe, naked pouring over his genitals whole box of powdered sugar. Sugar white air don't breathe, sugar floor astronomy. White both hands shaking.* That moves, that's a movie, *Alive*

Alive David's voice, speaking vowels, senseless out of the dark. Sound motion air. Alive. A photograph of this.

Albion now only a black wind. Audience now only photo of dark sound.

Somebody shaking my hand "shaking hands" my hands shaking, wants us both Albion and me to join her collaborate. This person wants to run ribbons of "Gwenna and David" through her work. Uses those names with her mouth. Uses word *ribbons.* When the person smiles at me, drained self-forgotten I smile back. I don't sorry have a phone I tell a man. Makes him impressed.

Black wind. People finally going away, black wind. Let's go get a bite black wind. Albion wretch mood *they didn't understand it* he says. *They came to be entertained.*

But YOU did great, he says. Threw away your script, huh. They loved you, so feel proud. (It's all right for you.)

Square building black marble. Gold door, no sign. He pushes right in.

I don't know what's wrong with me, he says.

We're in dark hallway, a cop in glass wall looks at Albion's membership card.

I feel sick, he says. I turned Gwenna over to those people. That's as bad as anything else I ever did to her.

Takes his shoes off, has me take off mine.
Room long narrow rosewood walls white carpet
tremendous thick soft. Malay about nine years old
boy glides fast without running mounting little
brown sticks in wall slots, low all around room. Lady
with hair pastille violet color kneeling on floor far
end. She's pulling silver bowls from down under the
floor, some freezer trapdoor below.

Boy starts putting flame to wall sticks, which
are purple sparklers. Lights go down.

Lights out. Purpled wall pouring fire out for
us. Boy lighting second wall.

We're lounging soft carpet floor before the
food lady, purple light her hair turned white floats
glowing how Albion's body lying in rug sinks.

He tells me: thought you could use some
dessert.

What I want: he tells the lady:

(whole room purple sparks boy now collect-
ing first already burntout sticks replacing with new
from apron and igniting)

want: those taffy candy things you guys
make here, taffy with the peanutbutter inside? *I love
those*. Put some in a tall glass, stick 'em to the sides,
line the glass with them. Put in microwave one
minute. Then put *hard-frozen* rum raisin icecream,
you have currants? OK raisins then, add raisins, and
chop up some cherries into pure Coke fountain
syrup, pour that over. And Jim wants, what.

Gloop sweet ice stuff always afterward makes

me sick. But I don't remember what I prefer. *Most people* love icecream. Audience loved "me."

I say: I'll have one of that thing you're having.

Malay boy sweating has a fever. The carpet is heavenly. Boy has to prepare our trays plus still renew on the run our sparkler light. I want to thank him but I'm a caption-writer. Gwenna in his pale purple face. Speaking is performing, I can't remember how I talk.

So he wastes himself on me. Each spark drawing itself dies. David within this tray: gentle arrangement exact drape cloth. Red lacquer tray: if it looks black it is black.

Pastille hair namebadge Elsie Mae withdrawn discreet. She's polishing a glass with piece of lace.

tall soft dessert all mine
I earned this
I REALLY SHOULDN'T
IT'S TEMPTING
I REALLY SHOULDN'T TAKE THIS

Into our sticky rewards, How's your weak stomach? Albion asks glum. Stronger yet?

When you get fat as me, he says, you can eat whatever you want. I feel sick I turned Gwenna over to people like that. Entertainment. I will never do this again (slurp).

I ate candy construct so quick I'm ordering another one. It's really really really sweet. Powdered sugar genitals black wind purple sparks, these become all stuck stopped. Breath unconstricts as you expand, my stomach. I even laugh at something he says.

No more pictures of David gnawing out his own liver I guess, he says and I laugh I want to not care.

You need a new subject, he says, that's easy. Everybody I know's got a crazy face.

Will I photo just anybody? Light pour lurid theatre sparks shift on face-suffering Malay. Albion voice out of lilac dark, Just look around.

Luxe carpet to the glow horizon. She's smiling at *me*, she's giving my second icecream. A fountain of love, nothing visibly wrong.

I take the camera off my belt clip, point at Albion he puts big sticky rum raisin hand over lens: No way, pal. No pictures. This is relaxing time.

He shouts Elsie Mae bring him a pot of hot fudge. He is going to demonstrate why audience got slightly bored with me at pictures 26 through 31.

Long spoon handle he dips fudge paint draws drip right on the white rug diagram:

Horizontal Lines like plot of novel, like time, time music melody, moves along in fudge drip lines of go and go and march-on-ahead. Very helpful fun to audience to take them by the hand and lead them along this horizontal brown easy path dribble.

Vertical Lines then disrupt drip up form a cage:

(I can't draw worth a shit, sorry)

(Eyes Malay won't watch rug to scrub)

audience slightly bored with me??

is where you're stalled piling up a meaning, chord depth philosophy but it don't *go anywhere* plump Albion sitting up vertical his palm up to heavens. Face full meaningfulness joke. Time burns dead two more sparklers.

I'm tedious and should be he. "You Jim need more forward movement to keep people interested. New meaning takes too long, try communicate with a known goal. Like political. Say like something that confronts AIDS. See, I did that, I had a dinner party against AIDS. Politics makes good food. People like when they already know what they think before they show up. It creates speed, fellowship. Did dinner party *opposed to AIDS*. Did dinner party about the Persian Gulf War—*opposed!* Served sand to gunpowder, oil to ashes. Theatre is church, like dinner. It's church, old rituals—people come to church of their fathers where they know the tunes. They want to sing along, they want to know already all about who is god."

Back in Albion's empty room the feather-dent sofa contour where Gwenna once was, empty. The newspaperman who does as he's told takes the picture captures sundown in Candyland. Sun a steady source orange window flavor piped-in. The bed motel shadow where Gwenna murderer dumb dead body did lie, *missing*.

Supply of continued light. A video machine would just suck images steadily. Never test itself.

Each next picture: small of her back smooth,

sunset light across, small of her back flesh is naked, porn lovely valley of orange.

Next each next want to photo each continue: hair disarranged like a guy viewer likes girl object hair, gold face hidden love ass, a still photo preserves protects, she's still with us. You say no corpse is sexy no corpse photogenic—just unsouled light returning. All the way from the sun to strike this.

But sun low. Light barely organizes, without light we can't think. I know what you mean you want objective light truth, I tell you that's just another technique but OK. I say I want to try everything, mean don't care I'll do anything. Cold strobe held up tilted down, prepared to blast out a sun-worth but only for 1/5000th second.

Sunset light and air, sunset a life to hold the strobe up within, strobe shape makes potatomasher sunset shadow on wall, my own arm shadow, same sun hits me and her both. See her through viewfinder ground glass: sun orange across even more soft, blood and floor all one mild color, corpse nice ruddy, not sex or even human but a place of quiet nature, stone beside a fence before hour magic twilight. And nobody can see what happens during 1/5000. And nobody can remember what happened during 1/5000. And take/*when eyepiece blacks out*/ FLASH returns me blameless sunset peace.

Later, treat the prints like thing separate. Across wood floor glare strobelight skin bits blood brown wash, one thin rope nice hair attached to

unattached scalp piece, the body gray-white
blotched red where skin smears forever against the
floor. Every wrong visible cold twisted against the
bed leg. Concentrate on color correction framing
effective presentation, this doesn't count, it's a *print*
now, not her life it's something I do. A rectangle
more important than temporary pain.

In icecream club Albion's just trying to help,
"my dinners make a holy moment where breath
stops—it's acting. You do that too. Photo is breath
stopped moment. Vertical. But *entertainment* starts
when you carry the folks *past* a bad moment to the
next *good* one. I fuckin TOLD you," he slaps the
camera out of my hand, it bounces into empty icecream glasses, "*no pictures!*"

(Let's get outta here, he mutters.)

But dark jumble behind icecream lady dark
wall, opening in wall he heads farther *in*. Albion
into dark gone.
     Why I follow him.
     Why I follow him. I don't know the way
back.
     Why I follow him, I already can't remember
his face. Why: my skeleton is too brittle. I feel it
cutting into me from inside. Mine could break,
break me with it, whereas his could be strong.
     Strong means his hate for me. His contempt
of Jim, which I share, could be love of "James

Chapman"—*cushion* skeleton—love not of me but what I would be immortally dead. My artiste worth extract. I am trying to sniff what he sniffs.

Step through lady break a dish, trip crash. Stump through curtain door hall black he's gone. Bleak sound of downpour, ceiling open, the hall an alleyway I'm *wet* getting *wet* rained on, run soaked toward (didn't retreat) distant light and faintest smell of burning.

Force through out of rainstorm to shelter curtain dazzle it's soft pillow ramp there's Albion already barefeet lounging calling me across the all-pillow drape-silk room, "You can't help yourself. I know! Me neither!"

The face I know. I'll try. My dying picture may develop in him. Face I know reach out his hand freeze my death.

David is running through the rain alone.

I fall wet down on silk sofa don't care what it does to the silk. Wet in a dry warm place. Cinema-scope fireplace burning hard like furnace. Parlor salon textiles ceiling, drapes sash pulls, soft sofas silk pillows. Rainstorm is an idea.

Girl ridiculous pasha orange costume shaven-head, razor nicks scalp, billowing chiffon, pale sweating, snaps her fingers. Albion grabs her by wrist, he knows what the fuck to do. Says "no, he's joining the club." She points face at, then looks at, then smiles at me. Smile impersonal grateful, like I'm vaguely famous.

She brings us to eat, because of who we are.

She has small cut on cheek, small cut on neck, bruise shoulder. Brings us big platters of what I can't look. Stomach torture throat squish-together ice-cream bile-tube airless lung sunless air.

No thank you. Nothing can follow icecream candy except Scotch: a filth-killing food which embalms the remainder. So the night never die. So a running wet man never reach ricochet.

Albion, he speaks. I see him alone. Photo is never of the taker. And eyes put in Albion's head so he could stare at a rectangle diagram. "This's a formal problem, that's all."

Gwenna pasha standing mid-room reaches her arms out—

"Beseeching sentimental."

Gwenna reaches her arms heavenward—

"Oh knock that shit off right now."

She lowers her arms. Her murderer is on the bed. Could be that's me.

"Why can't you underplay a little? Look at your boyfriend here. Look how cool."

Gwenna sits among cushions. She turns to my shotgun, which turns to her.

"This is a formal problem."

Shotgun rips cave in her face splatter—

He tears up diagram starts over. "Too Peckinpah. Emotion *and* integrity. Drama but soul. I shall overcome this difficulty."

His empty page is horizontal. Men and women in black hold black open umbrellas. Electric lights shine down on open dry umbrellas. Out in back somebody trying to play *Faust Symphony* piano transcribed, stop stagger clumsy. Center of group Albion, suffering monumentally disconsolate. The coffin's here too, shoved over to the side like buffet. Albion beautiful rigid with demonstrated suppression of misery throws one white flower down in grave hole.

David standing there like a dolt, looking out into audience. The makeup face minister hands David a plastic carnation and steps back to his tape mark on rug grass floorboard, the David actor just looks confused: "What." Albion perfectly continues vamp suffer while prompter whispers "Throw it in the grave. He throws flower in grave."

David, he thinks the coffin Gwenna box is *real*. Thinks she's really killed instead of art. Thinks somber is terror, instead of theatre. He breaks flower in halfstem, whips it at the prompter face, flies blind at space bright edge falls through down dark empty audience run limping up escape aisle. Voice yells "Don't break character!"

In the mourners stiffness goes flex, they drift away, and just the long cardboard rectangle coffin Gwenna dead: her mother small fortress steps over to me from the wings says (I'm lying there with the shotgun) "well how nice that you're here today. Gwenna'd've been tickled to death that you came."

Albion explaining everything tells me death's an *ultimate formal delimiter* hence a *portal of discovery*. So I look at this dead girl of his. Face down in coffin. Head is hair in little white ribbon bundle blonde. Back dead hair white dress. And I wait.

Albion shakes his head, shifts his diagram slightly, I go: "Oh...sorry...I thought you meant it was a portal of discovery for *her*."

To stay mud in soft silk cushion sofa kills people. I cannot bear to lie here. Yet Albion soothes me shouting nobody appreciates how difficult it is to stand up. "Bit off more than I could chew! Crit said it *ruefully*. Making the audience do too much of the work: should *assimilate* my materials first. Not spew out the INDIGESTIBLE INGREDIENTS. Hey you'll get bad reviews too, don't laugh—*you too* will remember every word. Guy in the *Gatekeeper Monthly* was not so rueful. Said I was shit. Said my work stinks. He really said that, 'stinks to high heaven, the work of a flatulent imagination.' That big bag of wind, I felt sick for days."

I'm up on hard back spine of sofa, my legs going up the tapestry wall, dripping Scotch into my mouth, start yelling "If David's an ingredient of mine, I'd want him dead tonight! Makes a better story! Dine out on suicide tales like *you*. But I got to remember..."

"Remember what?" Albion down on floor long low table oak slab he's drinking something white, eating big white custard, sliding ice cubes across the oak, hard, so they whizz into the fireplace and burn. "Fuck David if he can't deal. Ever read Faulkner about writing? Said 'Gladly rip out mah mother's guts t'get a good novel written.' If only it was that easy!"

Scotch, and the smell of burning dust. "Some idiot's playing a banjo in the building," I think I say I hear, up on hard spine back sofa avoiding soft cushions way way below, relaxed totally yet *by strength of soul alone* manage not fall down into lovely cushions. "He's out in the rain tonight running crazy because of me."

"Says, Faulkner, there's hardly any good novels, plenty of nice old moms. *Supply and demand.* And—we're lucky he thought that way."

"Why, did he kill his mother?"

Albion says "Your pictures of David showed like real limits of human emotion. They're cautionary. Important for posterity to see something like that. Could save a life a hundred years from now."

Albion says "Every time I do a performance about my father, I end big with food fight. Dad flips out raving. This is fun, it plays good. Audience likes it when a character *goes mad.*"

Albion says "You didn't fuckin kill him, he's paper you needed to use. *He's* not posterity. You make sacrifices yourself every day, you can't be responsible for every nutcase."

Albion says "All you did was tell the truth."

I'm in deep soft deep of sofa cushions pulling at cord weird fat green euro-payphone on wicker end table, trap with my drunk numb palms the Greater Candyland Regional phone book and pull it in front of my eyes. Sofa too soft to even sit up in.

Albion says "...don't die and don't stop. You know why I was able to do that dinner about Gulf War? Cause I didn't go *to* the Gulf War and get *killed*. Audience was uplifted by the one about AIDS, which I couldn't uplift them if I'd been dead of AIDS right? *Other* people die—"

Open two pages of phonebook biblepaper crumple fold force both to come to union. Take the name on left ISADORA stick it to the name on right NEZVANOVA call 911: *What is your emergency?* "fuck, sorry," click I meant 411: "What city please?"

"Candyland. The name is ISADORA/ NEZVANOVA."

"Checking...N-e-z?...I show no listing on an Isadora Nezvanova."

She's not born yet. Posterity, "but I need to talk to her!"

"I'm very sorry."

"*I'm very sorry!?*" Lady hangs up.

I can't shift. Close my eyes Scotch puts black rotating slicing blade behind my eyes. Black borders crepe around slicing blades. Can only listen not speak.

He says "She lived in a trailerpark in back of a bread plant—not a bakery, a huge factory for bread—us together in her trailer was the smell of that, she"

Says "beach South Carolina at night and phosphorous tides. Just talking holding on to each other, I was off my divorce. I was, yeh, happy. But—"

Says "...she's, dead. And I never got to say something good at the end. Good, I mean kind. To make up for horrible shit I said."

Says "But if you believe in images—if you can *invoke*—if you really believe that, then OK. You can fix things, some. You can create, and, destroy."

I hear him get up heavy, I squint: him limping leg-asleep to the dark behind empire of gold threads under my black skies chopping dizzy blades. A strange long time he's gone and when I grapple climb roll stand myself up out of sofa, fatter walk heavy push into the door men's room, there's Albion. Squat on the tile floor clutching his red-hot notebook writing writing.

Dinah I dream. Dinah dream on my head-ache kitchen floor barely moves. Sits clutching her stomach rocking back forth like a lump of food. I'm sorry I ate you

I'm sorry I hurt you. How is David?

(Lump says nothing. Don't hate me.)

(Says nothing. Please don't speak. Don't waken me!)

I'm saying I'm sorry, I say. How is David?

Dinah bleakest face. death

She speaks.

now you're going to publish those pictures

I babble into dream active, Listen! That

would be OK for both of us! A magazine's around
for a month, then it's gone! The pictures will go
away forever, see! I'm doing this on purpose! Is
David alive.

What's wrong with her face, now, only an
orange gloppy mask, fruit-pack skin peel disguise.
Nothing on the face under her mask appears to be
wrong with me.

David's fine, she says, *we're leaving town.*

Alive fine! Can I talk to him, I say, and:
Don't go. (I got away with it! Now give me love)

*I do not want to put him at further risk. Or
myself.*

She says it so tired it sounds easy, conversation. I start my set speech, my voice is junk metal
compacted junk being banged being slow lowered
banging into soundless mud, my voice, my individual voice is trash.

I want to treat you well in our personal moments.
in MY WORK I must *be exempted* from personal niceness
must be *ruthless* with me me and the world
cause see in the long run it's worth it as a portal

(Dream won't operate. Hangover eyes. Wide
empty opening in the dark.)

(Blank unhurt rectangle. I have to mark it up.)

(Across sheet of paper I write

Don't tell me, I know)

(now it's ruined wad throw it out window into courtyard junk.)

(Another blank sheet:

)

Knowingness when all has failed. Technique continues dry clicking parts fitting parts. Middle of my kitchen floor, alone at night, under my mattress: small tin covering. Open with can opener. Peel back tin. Black down there. Put my head. Crawl down inside. Because I own the things I know.

Dinner, late, her son away asleep. My doctor who never stops trying to cure me, love so annoying, has brought to table mélange rice millet beet carrot roughage. I'm trying to eat this *stuff*, I *am*, I'm trying, and she's not eating at all. Everything she does stupid and wrong. Deliberately insensitive to how irritating I find her. What's she trying to prove, not eating?

Lowering down self through dark tin bang hollow square tunnel black night I want to reach and photograph the main source pantry, crawl slip down grip to sides black into black. Tunnel QUITS: gripping to sides can't climb back up, I'm hanging kick, nothing.

Give up and drop.

"I gather you're not hungry?"

"I'm nauseated," she says.
"You're *joking.*"

HORIZONTAL:

"Well, I'm pregnant. That can happen if you're pregnant. It's a normal occurrence."

Give up and drop.

Give up and terrifying drop of 2 inches to stone ledge. Because I get everything for free. Trapped on a stone ledge, I feel down outerspace with foot. Another ledge right below. These are called steps. Step, down, feeling with feet. Head bump duck under stone ceiling I'm in cold stone chamber. Could almost stand up. No vision. Wall slots feel every few feet slot in stone. Five slots on each three wall. Fifteen stone slots stick head in each. Air rise cold from below. No light from below fifteen times. Make a noise *not*—fifteen times, each cold hollow *not* bottom echo distant.

If I don't say anything else. Revolve the words back inside, if I don't speak it might all get left at that.

My goal is to get away. Why say anything?

But I force myself spring the trap. Speak some sort of stuff "God, hell. I'm sorry. What are you going to do? You know, I'll pay for, for whatever—"

"*Don't*—worry about it." Clearing away dishes, clamp hands take mine away too, too many dishes in arms into the kitchen, dumping food in garbage, CRASH plates in sink, shout "It's got nothing to do with you."

Technique: I'd drown it dead with light. Downward metal passage gets five big floodlights. For stone chamber and steps, six umbrella lights blast away all atmosphere, all sense of depth, light into every cold crack. But slots down into unknown depth how the fuck do you light that?

How I love her to scream. Put herself in wrong, hah. *What* did she say? "What? You said. You're saying it's *not mine?*"

No other yelling from kitchen—she comes back sits at table. She says quiet right in my face:

"*It.* How could *it* be *yours*, Jim. What would make *it, yours.*"

"If I'm the father?"

"I do not say *it* is yours. I don't say I'm yours either, right?"

"Look, I'd help you in any way you want—"

"You are not a *father.* That should make you happy to hear. You're not *responsible.*"

"I'm not the father?"

"You are not *a, father!* I think you ought to go home now."

(I freeze. Is this possible? I could just walk out of story?)

Technique: run a long brown PVC pipe down chute right into stone chamber. Center of bright-lit stone floor split fat pipe into 15 pipe legs each plastic spiderleg running into its own dark slot: now I pump 6000 gallons of hot white chocolate down this pipe continue continue continue till every

possible unknown space is filled up. Take my time.
Allow to harden.

"Please go. Get away from here. Get *away*
from us. You're *off the hook, right?*"

In the face of her *unreasonable*
What more is there to
I am left with very little choice but
Silent walking out, I clench my teeth.
Moving through eight seconds of silence, five yards
to her door. Clench. Grimace, a grin. I must do this
alone. I am unsustained by the *voice that asks*. Voice
that asks asks: "You actually *left* her?"

Reply extremely lame: Well she said to.

Stomach. Worst. Downtown sitting against a
wall, so I can clench gut stone. Sweat and the
grimace. I'm free again. Grin the grimace. Across
street squint at world distant. World living-away
from me dying.

Out there across street, at base of chocolate-
kiss-shape streetlight, a girl sitting. Big cardboard
sign propped in front of her, behind the sign she's
reading a paperback book. Too quick turning pages,
I think she's reading back to front. The sign says
STARVING.

A tourist lady with two little kids, her
yellowdotted elastic-bag blouse says she's pregnant
again, stops speaks to the girl. Who looks up jerkily

and does reply but keeps on turning pages, glancing down, scared she'll lose her place. The woman gives the girl a couple dollars, then walks her kids on into the McDonald's.

Slowly girl stands up. She's really thin. Bent, red hands, red elbows. Hands shake, puts book in canvas bag. Cardboard STARVING clamped under scrawny arm, walks in McDonald's too.

In a minute I can stand up again. Weak I follow where girl went and startling inside, loud dozens of kids run chase around the circus-plastic walls, clutching bright paper cups of fry and shake. The parents sit at plastic tables, tables all too little for them, sit careful within tiny bright furniture, sit without talking. They eat tired, involuntary, how at work they down a coffee only for its dose of drug.

Starving girl orders, from pleasant tall button-face girl in paper hat, a Big Mac large fries and vanilla shake. Sits down with her orange tray beside a nursing mother, they nod smiles, and both women gaze at the fat baby.

On the wall framed paper sign in tiny type discloses fat content by dish. Big Mac 26 large fries 22 vanilla shake 10 total 58 fat grams. The nursing mother's having Happy Meal fat and sugar into nipple milk, the baby glue-eyed candified stupefied.

Starving girl eats very very slowly. Families come in and leave. She's taking one Mac bite each ten minutes. One sip white glop shake. One potato fry. Always in that order, will not desire. Getting thinner as she eats. Searching always through her falling-apart no-covers paperback, flip backwards and forwards never slowing down enough really to be reading.

I talk to the order girl with the paper hat behind the counter, order myself three Macs and chocolate shake, then say some stupid thing about fat sugar sodium content. Girl says, but that's what they want to eat! Then I ask her very loud if she's ever had a baby, and she won't talk to me anymore.

I leave her (the McDonald's clerk) (to die in childbirth) I go home fetch my videotape of the bug light probe outerspace-swimmer nosing inside my stomach. Because I have to see. Carry tape over to Candyland Audio play it back huge on their projector TV. Shoppers just look and pass by.

Suppose this is right now. TV show LIVE of my justeaten Big Mac milkshake soup. Suppose video probe looks says, no crime here. Just blameless health black walls.

Guy shopper staring up my huge mythological guts in awe, *bitchin TeeVee*, starts jabbing the buttons. Frame time freezes. My black stomach walls freeze I'm dead. Immortal, because in the future world a woman turns to husband and says, "He hurt me. Jim son-of-a-bitch."

I speak directly to David. Talking to my photo. This way can't hurt him.

Look at photo. Then scream at it and look. Then kiss it and look.

Throw photo out the fuckin' window, and see? it's *gone*. It doesn't fly back in and say "I thought we were friends."

Chef knocks at my sill. He was down in the courtyard: he saw photo litter flutter to earth. Came up fire escape to hand me it, "Hello my friend. You dropped this."

"Do you like it?"

He looks at me. "You *dropped* it. *Here.*"

Where you shine enlarger it's a negative, you have to focus, you can talk to it. "What are you thinking about? Are you thinking what I say you are?"

Stare turn bellows knob to blur-out. I have you, I can make up captions thoughts. But you aren't changed into what I make up.

Still don't know you any better. Hi Doctor.

Doctor's only a doctor in my head. SHUT UP just a memory woman voice I GOT AWAY. Tone of her voice. When I can't sleep I hear it, *at least I can't picture her*. But voice tone is her body and eyes, *let her die*. I'm yelling into my kitchen "DON'T TELL ME what's wrong with me! I already know! It's my stomach! It's my stomach, and wind-pipe, and large intestine! And my liver! Plus the heart and lungs! I am going to take care of it! I know what I need!"

Weigh myself. I weigh more in the day, but night always lose it. Got to eat hard just to keep myself. Stole a gram scale from downstairs, obviously must weigh food I eat, see what's going in, save feces and urine in orange vase and weigh that, write on chart subtract out vase weight, must know what I weigh. Gram scale becomes serving platter, chocolate cake from box to scale to mouth direct. Writing it all down even while next cake slice waits. Middle of night hours of sweating suddenly gasp realize and start scraping my sweat off with edge of a photo, weighing photo wet.

Pick slowly through rubble bits Dinah and David left behind, find one small white stone, not bigger than lima bean, white smooth stone mini potato in shape and I press into it my fingers, press it into my cheeks, then swallow it. Oh *no* forgot to weigh it first! Search rubble courtyard flashlight for nearest size pebble estimated weight.

Chart shows after eating rock, after rock passes through, my weight up one ounce. I assimilate stone.

Sunday morning 172 pounds 2 ounces. Sunday afternoon swallow a chrome-plated satisfying heavy metal bolt left from off Dinah's bicycle.

Somehow forget to weigh it first.

Guys twilight laughing out in courtyard. My window open, I'm lying on kitchen floor jaw biting to keep silent, but then it's quiet I think safe and I let long chord wrench scream. They hear me.

Guys I know from kitchen staff. Slow metal gong sounds up fire escape ladder, they put heads in window. Five heads ask me questions, then see I can't answer they stop asking. They come in the dark sweat-box and sit on floor all around me, they handle my containers see my prior shits, read charts of weight in three colors of magic pen, watch me sweat gasp fart slapping floor with palms of my hands.

Dishwasher kid of Ukraine says God sees your pain and rewards you for your suffering. Older salad man: Or the woman you love, even not knowing of your suffering she feels of it, maybe she now comes to you to love you in return. They discuss among themselves. All agree, in the long run this could make me strong, could make me happy. All agree something good comes.

(No I can't go. Congratulations. No. I'm

glad Albion you won whatever it is. No I can't deal with a dinner. No *you* don't understand!)

Jim come with me because friend, because support a friend. Go to a dinner could be helpful to you. Go *because* it's fake. Meet fake, learn about life. Go because free dinner free dinner.

(I'm not generous. I'm not your friend. I can't stand to watch you win some prize. I want my own prize.)

Now yr talking brother. Put on tux schmooze groundwork for monument to James Chapman—how you expect to win if nobody sees you, you dungeon.

(Your old tux? Am I getting fatter?)

Me in the mirror. Fat guy in my future. Bloat: TUXEDO: big MAN carry some weight heavy dude

Me with nothing. All burnt.

So yes: make new. Burn new.

Fuck everything. I almost fit in this glossy device.

I almost got to be well-rounded.

Candy is a fiction of food. I hurl Milk Duds one by one at dead kitchen of my ex-friends. Duds hit like click stone hitting a flat picture.

Picturesque in big flappy tux hurling stone.

Wearing his tux hand clutch Albion's own slippery jacket arm we walk out of town, down to the gatekeeper.

Down. Down to the gatekeeper.

You can't see the gatekeeper? You can't

see us walk down?

I have to draw a picture:

Invisible smoke-thick smell of burnt toast. Blacked rice pot-bottom like popcorn burn. Crisped-out meat fry charcoal layer smells of damage.

You can't see that! That's no picture!

Down sudden slope like near sleep first dream before you see you feel walking along sudden step *down*—you *jounce* in the bed like dropped a foot—wakes you up into black room.

Nothing to show for this.

Gatekeeper. You know what an obstacle is? You know jumping through hoops?

The crook dark arm of my supposed friend.

Invisible. Because I have nothing goodbye,

THE END

Dear _____.

The flesh of the gatekeeper face is like pink spun candy. Do you believe that?

The flesh of the gatekeeper. Is pink spun candy.

When I say "I'm sorry" you don't believe me, this is a novel I'm hiding behind a character. I'm sorry.

You could believe me and it not help.

I make strange self-hurt gesture with my arm, standing in front of the gate, gesture means forgive me. Print it in a thousand copies, the awk-ward arm twist a thousand times, forgive me a thousand times. Go on a talk show apologize "look how I've multiplied my sincerity image!"

So I have some profit even if you continue to despise me. And profit is

The gate Mexican skull-angels hammered in black iron posing as nine Muses. See them. Gold-fang gargoyles on top gate spikes.

So you can see. So I can demonstrate visibly. Details are additional little gifts. Propitiate reality weight to make the offering.

There's actually nothing in my hands.

Five hundred pounds of strawberries in a metal box, slow white smoke coming off them. High-voltage cable leading out of box through grass away down the road. Smell of air strawberries electrocuted intense as eating, makes saturating hunger, every pore now desperate to suck strawberry.

Did we get through the gate? Never saw it open.

Certain things missing. Leaving out little words rescue me fires of hell. So you won't understand apology.

You won't read this book anyhow. We'll agree to never mention.

You aren't reading this now.

So I'm alone here. A row of flatbed horse-wagons, me and Albion climb aboard one says PIES red paint edge letters.

I'm alone of you. The driver of horse is

wearing a large cardboard costume.

It's addressed to you and you will not read it. So what is it?

Thing; novel; ship in a bottle. Chocolate-colored mare in yellow harness, yellow reins back to piewagon driver.

Write something you *would* love me for again if. In a big glass jar two little men in tuxedos. Toy wagon, toy plastic horse, the driver is a candybar. How did I get this toy stuff through narrow neck of jar? That's what counts, the trick. It could be any junk inside jar, a box of instant potato flakes. Amazing trick is amazing.

Mr. Goodbar six-foot cardboard-box yellow candywrap holding yellow reins, we ask him his name in there and he won't step out of character, "Mr. Goodbar, sir."

Amazing trick's a trick. Bottle's empty. Roll up a photo of hillside scene. (Maybe you visited a hillside once, once in all your life, just to take the picture.) Paper photo dry rustling sound, stick through feed jar mouth fill with artificial world.

Albion shouts at driver if he's hot in that candybox costume he's wearing, hey haw haw you must be *melting*, I look away other hillside. Next tin box of electrocuting food approaches for odor silent firework decoration nothing smell. Nothing smell.

I can't smell it.

I do not see the valley into which I descend.

Dear _____,

There's a big party to tell about, then try to finish up. Then you don't read it anyway.

Glass jar with the picture inside, me and my fat friend in tuxedos descending into unseen valley in a piewagon driven by hands and legs of a chocolate bar, our faces are vapid little weddingcake plastic grooms. And black finger-paint letters Hölderlin quote smeared around the outside of the glass jar world TO LIVE IS TO DEFEND A FORM.

Dear _____.

I can't defend or explain what I did. [Proceeds to defend, explain.]

With all my love and incredible moral integrity, I remain

St James

Always felt opposite about forms. Seems awaker to attack your own given form, attack what you naturally do well, what seems easiest "you," what might get praise for its steadiness certainty. Accept no prefab self-power. Want to break that to find what I *can't* do, what I suck at, so learn what was defensible among now broken pieces.

Could be true of friendship, form of friendship. Make it new for truther truth. Damage out its rote shape, attack it where easily achieved.

Have done good job so far.

Want to insist fucking up doing what I don't

know how. Be sure fail *notably*. Then any residue praise true love for "me alone."

Brilliant. Who loves you like that.

One person. (Not pictured here.) I write for her.

I'm that lucky.

Will not write about her.

(She might want me to finish this...?)

NO ☐   YES ☑

(She says she'd like to see my face.)

Can't you...? Didn't I—

Plastic cake-boy face, oh.

Plastic cake golem with un-face whimpers "I can't see, can't sniff, hey."

I can't do self-portrait: evade into cartoon bully safely worse than any self. Try to tell what really happened I jam up in flawed-tough mask hiding obvious other face Pre-Raphaelite shadow. Up above my swoon two Jims float feeding each other angel-cake.

Electric char of cake waste carbon sugar wrenches my face up wrinkles. Somebody doesn't want to want angel-cake. Albion says the air tastes great...him in the piewagon beside me big fat gulps of ashes air, he's awake at least and multiplied, there's other tuxedo men walking across the green slope below, each thing I see is a wish to see the next, write down even for my old betrayed friend to never read, even for the word thing picture itself, for smells of cantaloupe and gasoline, for pyramid of burning apricots, for the raked-together pile of bay leaves smoke smoldering, for the autumn burn off other piled distant spices, I pick out nutmeg char and smoking celery, sniffing even if sniffing hurts somebody, even if it makes me so much worse than ever, do want to sniff and I do sniff.

Albion slapping my back, hey boy so you decided to get over it! Time to *produce*—

A great multiplication of piewagons, all leading down this slope of grasses into smogyellow valley. Multiplied fires, haze of heavy all-flavor smoke sugary meat taste. Bunches of identical little tuxedo people. Fertility, yells Albion, footwork! Bury the folks in your shit!

All the other wagons are full of pies, the people are laughing pie-eating. We have no pies. Albion immediately leaves me, jumps down runs cross-slope to green wagon with lone tux-drag woman eating whole pies, they together eat the feast of smog valley pies of sweetmeats, pies quince and elderberry and hazelnut in custard, pies roast squashflowers in lime, they have every pie in multiple and me no pies at all.

Banners of red silk in white letters pass overhead

HERE'S YOUR REWARD

then a few yards later down slope

FOR WORKING SO HARD

On my back in the bare wood wagon I'm smiling. No trouble breathing, gut really not too bad. Rattle shake of wagon joggles me within baggy tuxedo, cradle soothing approval.

Albion careering ahead smeared with pies, his voice I hear near ear low like a prompter: *I love an apocalypse at the end—turn the tables over, explode it up with smoke canisters and electric blow-up noise—every time I get to destroy the whole world—the whole world I destroy—*

A field planted with living plants. Half a mile flat across valley farm plants. Even in brown food-smog after-sundown darkening huge haze ceiling, rows flutter plants deep green. It is not obvious what the plants are for.

A house far off tiny down hill across field.

We arrive at valley flat, not part of farm field, swamp water. Taller grassy plants wet below and burnt-dry on top. Look straight down in gray diffract water I see the whole purpose of these, they are weeds working to produce next weeds. Tuxedos forgather. A woman in low black dress flesh of her breastbone exposed, this breastbone is indented, a small cave. Indent could half hold contents of a gravyboat. She's treading mud holding high a quilt of lurid scraps. Swamp grass muds her black hem rasps her bare legs. Tuxedos collect at a long table in the weeds, men and women stained yellow laughing, sucking in air, praising the savor, multiples retch choking.

Seated dinner party of one hundred in murk swamp ice darkness, light shines up from the food, *sorrel soup with figs and dates* the light from soup-bowls up into these hungry faces, light lost above them in yellow smoke, soup-light never reaches farther high than low black clouds of valley night *spiced chestnut cream* people dip their hands in tureens of goop, everybody talking at all times, each performs his specialty, poets pout aloud and painters describe shapes in the smoke *almond curry omelette* woman with indent made her art quilt out of her mother's metaphor breast cancer says she, spreads it over the heads of other speakers and keens her mother's maiden name in bel canto *brie tartlets in lemon malt* the sleet slush bits fall bright into foodlight, the sleet fallen through darkness smoke is flavored with the smoke of all flavors, sleet into open upended mouths of eaters. A waiter touches the head of fat very young man sculptor talking gallery gossip, talk his art, he's mixing plate foods together sculpting for all-flavor, the sleet in his cold hair crust melts all at once when waiter leans over accidentally rubs his head, that young man's eyes close in ecstasy *spiced toasted marshmallow with almond dust* when I touch the flesh arm of the dented quilt woman she gasps midsentence talking now talking smiling *swan neck pudding with roses and mustard///artichokes with blueberry rice///fried valencia oranges*

Far downtable Albion throwing confetti shreds back up at the sleet. These white little paper slips like cookie fortunes flying across table everywhere, caught in food sodden, diving wet off table blowing at damage crawl away from us across freezing-over swamp.

Dry underneath the table of centipede

knees, two hundred shoes. It's warm and muffle quiet here. Heat rises from one square in center, an open book. Cat with orangeblack lynx ruff flattening open heat-source book with one paw, rips away pages with teeth. Confetti by thousands she creates shredding with chew, but always spitting *pah* always spitting out.

Tick clicks. Gray ice tidbits landing on our plates, tinging rim into china bowls of sugared cream, little gray hailstones suddenly increase music off silver and china bells, so everybody stops talking and listens to the chord arrivals. The confetti shreds of paper all over our table now getting shuffled by rattling attack hail. Paper word book shreds show bits of sentence,

> *burlap ball is warm*
> *she's gurgling at the ceiling*
> *ladyfern unfolds*
> *shard of window glass at her mouth*
> *light glow in wet grass*
> *blinking squinting twitching*
> *furry face of the white fungus*
> *she rolls into a mudball*

These words—hail hits these words. Hail hits paper making holes. Hail bounces the little words to gray. Hail gnaws the dead book to pulp.

The clink of hail hitting teeth of one hundred diners, their heads all back now mouths open manna. Under table now flooded frozen swamp, cat escaped gone, book no words remain empty covers locked drowned under ice. Guests all so happy, big

mouths piled stopped overflowing with tasty gray
hail, eyesockets gray pyramids, laps filling up.

I don't feel it. Don't feel the cold. See hail
bounce off my face and hands, nothing.

Pick up tiny boulder of hail from the tablecloth, put it on my tongue. Pork intensity, agoniz-
ing. Another gray bit: hideous concentration of
butterscotch.

This is all I've eaten all day! I want to tell my
friend how pure I've been. Walk over to Albion's
chair. He doesn't move. Jaw pulled down gape.
Mouth eyes stopped all ice.

I tug a little his ice-weight beard. Don't want
to be without him. On my knees in ice mud, whis-
pering in his bright red ear "Today I hardly ate
anything."

He shudders slight all over, his chair tips
back slow fat ice man weight all falls backward into
mud. I'm grappling him to rescue and all the hailstones in his mouth he suddenly spews right in my
face, ice that sticks to me, *roaring*, roaring he's
laughing, and shouts, hands gripped strangle around
my neck, "*Ain't you hungry?*"

Yeah...I'M STARVING!

He pulls me we're both laughing away from
table through crazy hailstorm up a dead ridge
toward the trees, there's old wooden shed he yells
pantry! we're ready to bust down door but door just
opens to admit, we rush into silent dark—start
opening crates of candied figs each fig in its own
little slide-open paper matchbox, we chew up the

crunch gummy things and scatter boxes around the dark, attack rip apart a rope-hung medicine-ball-size wheel of wine-sweetened cheese, stab out paraffin seals on widemouth jars of red-syrup green berries, human hands designed to grab, a pine crate of thousands of sugar wafers, finally enough sugar wafers! then an open steel tub of eels and minnows in mint aspic, this is incredibly almost like real nourishment, stunned greenmouthed with minnows I look around for more meat. It's cold in here. *Meat* is the cure, horizontal cabinets, pull handles out, horizontal drawers old walnut out of the wall, Albion throwing pottage at my back of head, this heavy long drawer lined with glass, slopping full of brine and a whole cleaned porpoise ready for in-skin Hawaii roast. We together pull the beast out of bed into our arms and standing up just start biting into the slitopen innards, staggering dancing, silver flesh on outside sleek sexy to grip and drips down our shirts fishwet smell of mammal and peppers, the brine tastes of Mexican chili, pepper makes harsh thirst and the fish sweet juice quenches, my eyes tears burning running salt over the pink Aztec fish meat. When Albion sneezes lets go his grip on her I can't stay dancing, trip over the heavy tail and fall right out the door of the shed. I'm *safe* because I fall within my big fish, the hail carpet rolls me on it like marbles, slide slow me inside porpoise together down the little hill, I'm still eating because I'm still hungry, slide together down into deep and cold swampwater. Albion splashing in trying to save me, grabbing, pulling, but if I keep quiet I'm warm in the fish, I won't be rescued.

Chewing.

Gnawing, chewing.

Slowly, swamp ice muck edges into the flavor.

Slowly, I do not want any more.

It's dark in here. I can't move.

Cracking sound when I shift my head. Nightmoon light. The fish is half-shell empty, most of the flesh weight on me is Albion. We're trapped in the ice. My teeth are sunk in the nape of Albion's neck.

The wind whip cold over my face and teeth. Eyes still watering; I see the table of iced-over guests dead stopped, I see the picture of that. See the ploughed field stretching green away, little house off away far, picture. Can't see how I myself look.

The cold glues up my eyes. The wet of my eyes is colder thick. When I'm frozen shut I will not see. At least will not see.

So I don't see. Frozen. I don't describe anything and there's nothing at all.

(Dark.)

(But wind. The sound of wind. The cold of wind)

Wind. World's not destroyed. I freeze away but no apocalypse. Curtain doesn't rip top to bottom. It's only me made nothing.

One last stomach gurgle, and become broken camera body. Some film went through it once.

Is this apology indigestion too oblique?

Gwenna I didn't even bother change her name. She really was once girlfriend of mine, really was, though many years later, killed by shotgun. I'd be free to write whole books about her forever without hurting her at all (any worse) she being dead. But being dead she's not my type subject, refuses to paradox, she lacks my fabulous flexi-moral imagination. All she wanted to do was live.

But apparently I'm free to write anything about anybody anyway.

Barely managed to keep my (actual relative) out of this story—who nearly threw self off a steeple, then nearly overdosed pills. *True story* I thought it'd be a neat idea write a short book about, so I did but didn't publish yet. Reading that (even reading these lines here now) might make (actual relative) kill himself for real? "We can't save him," my (other relative) said, "and we can't kill him," saying which lie we felt better. Us feeling better was the main thing.

The little book about him's pretty good. I guess it'll go out someday.

You know you someday got to die, you got to die, you got to lay down and

One girlfriend once, her little brother hung himself. I wrote that right into the novel I was working on, then gave it to her to read. Apart from that though, how'd you like it? Was it *strong*. It keep you *interested*.

Dear _____ : maybe you're how you pretend with me, *interested* in discussing abstract "general issues" like betrayal. Maybe you're interested in this book's general issue, but you find it, like those of my others you've read, too dithered-out fake avant-vague. You might like a short story called "Kumiko" by Naoya Shiga. Narrator playwright decides his writing's gone stale, he has an affair with an actress merely to make his life interesting enough again to write about. And though this causes his wife to swallow poison and die, it also means he's able to write a very successful full-length domestic play with lots of verve.

Shiga also wrote a novel once where the husband leaves his wife simply because he'd rather live awhile in the mountains alone. When the wife finally comes to visit, to tell her husband she submits to his sadistic wish to abandon her for this indefinite period, she finds him lying sick in bed surrounded by large flat beetles crawling. The husband says, referring to these beetles: meet my friends, my only friends.

This Shiga wrote a lot about crawling bugs. Bugs instead of wives, bugs instead of people. You'd like those books better than this. In those books there's nothing of you.

I disguised you pretty clever. Nobody'd ever guess this book's about you two.

Except you yourselves. You would guess.

Obvious to you. I did forget to protect either of you.

Good thing I wrote this tearful apology! Take my picture now? Looking like this? Then we both agree for you to hate me. I'm slowly curing myself of my stupid idea you'll respect me hugely for all this fuckaround. This very book compounding original crime making it *much worse* between us just when we were getting along OK again—you'd basically forgiven me I think. Last week you phoned me for help, for cheering up, for advice.

Selfhood: a gig. A bit. Self-expression at all costs. *You* could write something about *me* then. We can be pemmican chew for each other. Write rotten about me, writer. You're free to. We all can have great lives.

The thing is to keep finding reasons to put words. If I can't take people I know and attack portray, what's *my style my voice*

shuddering
"shuddering": for effect
shuddering actual worse
without stop.
to no end
Narrate.
after
word
otherword
after novel next
hurts stinks pain in eyes
what can I give you
here   here

here   take
won't have a voice
voice throat burnt
voice gutmuscles torn
voice tongue swelled
empty
won't have throat
won't have breath
yours all
not describe belly revolt
no picture green face
no sound purging
no wave puking
no evoke puke ink over ice
no equate puke endless sermon
I'll expel   will you accept
Haw haw course not!
*Your friends are already lost to you. Continue
your work.*
who

■ ■ ■ ■ ■ ■ ■ ■ ■ ■ ■ ■ ■ ■ ■ ■ ■ ■ ■ ■

The air was clear. Ice melted generally across
the valley. A banquet table heavy with piled ice,
white high pyramid on table legs, sank slowly into
the thawing mud.

Across the potato field, in the dark, one
window showed lit in the farmhouse. White smoke
spun up out of the stovepipe, lit yellow by
windowlight as it sank back slowly in the warm air.
This was the only smoke in the valley.

On the ridge opposite stood one man in a tuxedo: a hired entertainer. He was waiting for the guests who, however, had all sunk away. On his dark ridge he tilted his head back to the sky. Raised his sword to the sky. A hero, somebody with a plan! But then merely pointed his sword at himself, metal sliding into his mouth, stopping his voice, merely swallowed his own sword. Made a show of this. Impaled, he flourished arms out, he bent forward in a stiff bow. All his eyes could see was the black sword handle in his face.

Then he stood and unsheathed. Lack of audience made him need dinner, so he walked away.

Across the ridge near the pantry shed, a thing of mud moved in the mud. It unfolded, rose up to stand, as if mud attained a spine. Walked, mudman, through the dark down the ridge to the edge of the potato field. Huge field, huge sky, tiny distant house, Jim mudman.

Jim, mud already drying on him and, where he flexed, dropping off him in brown worms, Jim mud. Jim started his march across the field. Jim treading on not one plant, walking straight line along a muddy irrigation ditch. He was smaller than a single tree in the forest behind him, he was smaller than the tiny house that never came any closer. Bogged down and fell.

Retched, an effect of the clean air. But he had nothing left in him.

The whole black night huge, every part of the night holding itself distant from every other part. The forest was lit up with little yellow flickers.

Jim slowly walked back out of the field and up through waste mud into that forest. Disappeared.

Now nothing moved but the far meal-stove smoke farmhouse and the flutter of lights on fir trunks.

After time the smoke stopped, thinned out into dark. Then nothing around the farmhouse moved.

After time the candle flicker on the treetrunks died out, tree by tree. Nothing in the forest moved.

A large red rock in the clearing by the pantry shed. Bones of a huge fish half buried in the mud. The fish, killed by a fisherman, once swam, now an image. The red rock to never move did not require pre-murdering.

Jim was moving invisible around the forest. In Candyland, Miss Nobel slept alone. She looked dead still but she was breathing, was moving, blurring.

The mud dead fish, fixed.

The farmhouse of killed wood slabs.

The wood slabs pantry shed.

Wide dark of the valley slid with air. Forest grew and rattled leaves. Potato plants bereft in rows but quivering. Ripped flattened floor of ploughed field blurred through spinning night planet space carrying its bits of bug and leaf carcass. Each bug and leaf, dead, lived its life out first.

Inside the forest, one hundred little round

dead-cedar-slice tables had been set out among the
fir trees. Each table with its own white candle in
blue glass cup.

Jim walked through the forest from table to
table, looking for his own.

Each table with a propped metalframed
photograph. Each table photo a different face, face
always looking right into its camera, open faces dead
still and a candle burning.

Each table also offered dessert: a little glass
of two-layer custard and a silver spoon.

Jim, looking at the face of a woman stranger
standing in a bedroom filled with paintladders and
dropcloths, she looking back at him like about to
laughing sing, took up the custard to taste. Top
layer white creamy feeling in his mouth, utterly no
taste. He ate and ate trying to find anything to it,
wondering did he burn away his tastebuds, then he
hit the black bottom layer.

Black pudding, it knocked him down. On his
hands and knees, eyes shut. Falling over on his side.
Face like suicide. Still clutching on spoon and glass.

He lying on his back took another bite.
Screamed.

Sweat. Forced himself up kneeling. He found
the table edge with finger clutch.

Stared at the still photograph.

After time Jim had visited each of the
hundred tables, looked at every victim photo, taken
up every spoon. He flicked the white stuff into the

dead floor needles, white just diluted the full taste of the black. Candles were dying by the 70th table, had to look at pictures by flicker of few remaining candles. One of these last tables, with its picture of Albion's Gwenna, Jim spent no extra time here. He was the only guest in the forest, he had to serve everybody.

Final table reached as the last forest candle died. Effortful squinting only showed him a framed area of black picture. Decided to treat this as his table. The picture would be of Dinah and David then. This black area was any picture Jim once took and later tossed out for being too calm, too relaxed, "ordinary," subjects trusting the photographer.

For this table Jim ate slowly all the white then savoring slowly the black, every bit of the black, now able to stand up under the hideous taste, tried to hold it around his tongue and make it bad as possible. The mouth can taste even with the gums, the throat walls know when something tastes extreme, the length of foodpipe feels it, the stomach for courage grips itself. The bitterest taste outlines the whole inward eater to himself.

Beyond the hundredth table was forest dark. Jim walked directly into the dark. Immediately slammed against a wood wall.

Slam like one drumbeat out into the dark.

Jim was at the wrong end of the valley. This he'd run into was the little far farmhouse. The potato field stretched *behind* him now, though he never walked across it.

Jim was a tiny bug on the land. The house a little cube.

Light came on in house. Light glow surrounded by mud. Mud and smell of farm shit, wet asleep pigs wet silent dirt. Jim wandered the ground examining dirt feel, shit clay food dirt he rubbed on his forehead and cheeks. Rubbed it into holes of his nose.

A woman's head stuck out the door. Their words slid easy on the wind.

Dinah's voice: We don't think about it anymore. That's over

Jim's voice: I'm doing fine. No problem

Dinah came outside, they stood together, Dinah shining a flashlight at his chest, talking.

Jim's voice: How's David.

Dinah: Fine.

They looked by flashlight at a pile of drawings Dinah was holding. Jim taking examining each like a diamond merchant.

Jim was shouting, waving the clutch of pictures around, "it's not fair! he has an advantage! he's suicidal! that's a gift!" Dinah reaching to take the pictures back, they blew out of Jim's hand and made white clipped wings flying in swooping slices across the field, till each stopped by a plant then hopping row to row with the wind gusts.

Dinah stood eyes shut. Jim standing there who lost all these drawings of theirs, who didn't know what to do with his hands or how to just stand there and watch the white squares blow away, Jim reached down took a clod of her earth, pitched it over to her, his voice dimly "target practice." That must have meant something. Perhaps it meant she should *catch* the dirt clod and *throw* it at some target, whatever target appeared ready to receive dirt—the dirt hit her in the mouth. Sputting and Jim yelling *aw woops*, but Dinah grabbed hurled dirt *bang* hit Jim on the side of head, dirt not flurrying in a little cloud but payloads heavy thudding clay, hit Jim on chest, on legs, in center of face. Jim who was already mudman, Jim who'd already smeared himself everywhere. She stopped. Her dirty hands were held out open like they must not now touch anything. *Keep on* Jim said, she was walking back in the house, *keep talking* Jim said, she went inside and shut the door.

Beautiful drawings were blowing in the potato field, but Jim was at the window yellow light, trying to look in. Couldn't see his friends. All he saw was a little square wood frame inside high on a wall. In the frame rows of things gray and brown, these were moths on pins. The yellow light went suddenly out; Jim's eyes dilated wide.

He could hear their voices inside.

Sat in the dirt yard bent clutching stomach, mumbling

I'd never be able to eat this food they make out here.

The sound coming from a pyramid of potatoes in the barn. Sound of waiting.

*If I could make something. If I could farm.
Maybe I could eat.* The shed, the barn, the cow barn,
the fence to the west field (corn) the fence to the
east field (alfalfa), the farmhouse and the potato
field.

It would have made a better STORY if
David had killed himself. But he did not. The story
suffers, suffers. Life is full of suffering.

Ground filthy hands into his pockets, *I could
do this. If I had to. This ain't so much of something.*
Walked bigger steps across the yard, hands out in
air, hands dancing up, open, then closing taking.

A feller's got a job to do, he does it.

His "hick" accent very poor

*See all that land out back? Nice spread huh. All
that was forest, son. I bulldozed them trees. Burned off
the little stuff, ploughed the ashes under, smashed up
them big old stones into road gravel. OK? Got me a tree
shredder machine too. Runs on gasoline. Gasoline, that's
just old food.*

Jim very small on the landscape

*Man's gotta make a living. Farming it all
depends on you, got to get up at 4:30, no playing
around. It's not something you pick and choose, like
saying I don't feel inspired just today, them cows are
inspired up with milk regardless.*

Jim city nambyfiction softboy shouting to
nobody, making it all up

*I let that fence go, and guess what. Three cows
busted it down last week, got in the corn, they ate and*

ate. Swelled up with gas, died. Stomachs ruptured.

yell as loud as you can, still

There's outfits'll purchase a cow in that condi-tion! Still plenty of use for a cow like that!

who knows his facts from mental math, draws pictures with his fists

One potato is lunch, ten thousand potatoes are agribusiness! If nobody buys my food in time

who does not learn

they'll buy the next guy's! Mine rots and the BUGS, *the* BUGS *eat it*

who destroys to purify

me alive in the fat of all who need me!

who don't know how to grow!

my creation's got to be swallowed or I disappear

Jim dark against the dark, black stomping blackness

seen everything, lived right past other people's deaths, I was the first cowboy. I fought and killed the SHEEP MEN, *sheep crop grass and good cattle starve, one food destroys the other, before sheep* STAMPEDE *me they'll* DIE FIRST

does not know who he is

what the hell is that?

maggots. gonna turn to moths. did you bring your camera

if you gonna puke you do it like a grown adult. take this shovel, dig up a hole. hold it back while you dig. now you ready, puke go ahead.

all right   now cover over what you done. give
the black stuff a good burial

    you still look sick

    Lying on his back. What work it was to put
himself here. Lying on his back, the dirt ditch shape
like a cradle. And potato feather leaves in the wind
chiffered beside him, a row left a row right, him in
the ditch between, where mud runs.

    David and Dinah ploughed this line and
planted the thousands of plants each at separate
gesture. They did the work, and Jim didn't.

    An unprotected plant he grabbed, dug his
fingers in and pulled root. Up came a dangle of
black dirt weights on strings, a potato in each one if
he would clean it off to see.

    Now this bunch couldn't grow anymore. Did
they know yet they were dead?

    Potatoes, dirt weight on his chest in the
dark. With his fist he crushed against himself, but
could not grind to pieces, one unripe, uncooked,
cold green stone potato.

    Crawling across his cheek, an independent
life. He put his finger to it and it lumbered aboard,
he peered: bug like a tiny black armadillo, droop-
ended and all self-contained.

    He puffed air on it and it curled up in a ball,
a perfect round marble immediately rolled off his
finger and somewhere in the black ditch lost. Jim
searched and searched for his friend, then found

another bug on the back of his hand.

It crawled around to the bowl of his palm. With fingertip Jim tapped it. It rolled up, he rolled it around. Then waited, waited long enough, the potato-bug forgot and unrolled, went walking across his palm.

Tapped it again, it balled up round. Jim rolled it carefully onto the dirt ridge beside a stem of potato herb. But in accident it rolled on all the way down into Jim's ditch, horribly vanished into a crack in the earth.

Waited. Waited long enough. The potato-bug crawled back up out of the earth, slowly headed up the side of the ditch. Jim squinting could see it reach a large lightcolor clod of dirt halfway up, a plateau.

On this plateau was another bug, stranded on its back, rolling and unrolling, waving its legs in the air. "Jim's" bug came over the edge of flat ground and walked directly over to the stranded one. Jim waited to see his bug help the other to its feet. Instead, his bug bit off one of the waving back legs and ate it.

Attacked bug rolled up, but, wounded, could not roll tight. Unrolled open again. Its friend bit off another of its legs.

Jim tapped the leg-eating cannibal and it rolled up a perfect sphere, beautiful armor-tight. Jim lifted it up, popped it in his mouth.

Brushed the wounded bug down into the crack in the earth, I'm sorry, good luck, I'm sorry.

Carefully re-planted the potatoes he'd yanked up. The potato plant sat there, plausibly. Evidently would survive, to be eaten later.

It was night. A pig was dreaming of a whole mighty tree uprooted with his one nose.

Night. A cow dreamed machineless open grass and silence.

Jim asleep in the field dreamed one perfect white potato he could eat. Dreamed eating it, bite by bite. Seeing all this pleasure on his own face, wondered why he couldn't taste.

And someone young in his dream took him by the hand, led him behind the shed to show him all the potatoes he had rejected, the imperfect ones. They were dark down thrown in a dug pit, rotting already, covered over with red tiny spiders.